FROM YOU TO ME

FROM YOU TO ME

K.A. HOLT

SCHOLASTIC INC.

ISBN 978-1-338-27764-7

10 9 8 7 6 5 4 3 2 1   18 19 20 21 22

Printed in the U.S.A.   40
First printing 2018
Book design by Baily Crawford

Dorothy Parker once said, "This wasn't just plain terrible, this was fancy terrible. This was terrible with raisins in it." This book is for anyone who has experienced terrible with raisins in it. It's a fancy terrible fist bump, from me to you.

CHAPTER ONE

TAYLOR SLAPS HER HAND ON her hip, the smack echoing through my bedroom. "I look good in these pants."

"You are a loony toon, Taylor." I hop into my matching pair, yanking up the zipper.

"Well, then I am a loony tune *who looks good in these pants.*" We stare at ourselves in the full-length mirror on the back of my bedroom door, lost in our own thoughts for a minute. When did Taylor get taller than me? I move my palm in a straight line from the top of my head and it bangs into her forehead. Taylor laughs.

"Okay, then." I lean over and grab a black T-shirt from the pile of clothes we've been trying on since seven a.m. I pull it over my head and say, "We're going to walk down those halls and every mouth in

Hemingway Middle School will gape open like that singing fish in your dad's office."

Taylor pulls an identical shirt over her head and tucks it into the identical black jeans she's trying on.

"I mean, you know what Beyoncé says."

Taylor raises her eyebrows in a mock questioning look. "Who run the world?"

"Girls."

"No, but *who* run the world?"

"GIRLS!"

We admire ourselves some more. All black. Yes. This will show the school that we mean business. This will tell everybody that summer is over and Amelia and Taylor are ready to take over the world. Top-dog eighth graders, that's who we are.

Taylor twists her long curls and spins them up to the top of her head. "I look like Sandy. Not even close to Beyoncé."

We start singing "You're the One That I Want" from *Grease*, both pretending to be Sandy from the end of the movie, when she's had her black leather transformation.

"You girls about done in there?" The annoyed voice calls over a loud knock on the door. "You don't want to be late on the first day!" Mom was a little grouchy about having to wake up so early to let Taylor in this morning. But then, thankfully, she realized the importance of getting our first day of school outfits *juuust* right.

"Almost done!" Taylor giggles.

We do some last-minute shirt tucking and walk out of my room and past my mother, whose face always looks pained these days. Mom hands us both breakfast bars and we grab our schoolbags. Taylor whispers, "Who run the world?"

I smile and hope that all the joking and singing has worked as some kind of magical camouflage. If I act happy, I will be happy. If I tell myself I'm happy, I will be happy.

I will be happy.

I will be happy.

CHAPTER TWO

SOMETIMES WHEN WE DRIVE BY the lake, I think I can hear it growling. Is that crazy? I see the dark stillness of it spread out along the horizon and I wonder if maybe under that peaceful surface is the whole body of a monster. Its head is turned up to face the sky, its mouth is wide wide wide open like that one time I watched a rat snake eat a baby possum. The monster is waiting quietly, patiently, for its next meal. I press my ear against the window of Old Betsy and I hear the rattling of her rusty doors and the whining of her all-weather wheels, but I also hear something else. Something low, almost more of a feeling than a sound.

The lake is hungry . . .

It's been three years since its last meal . . .

"Amelia." Mom's golden eyes, her tiger eyes, dart up to the rearview mirror, catching a glimpse of me in the back seat. "Amelia. Are you okay?"

I don't answer. Taylor looks me over and seems to decide that I'm probably okay. She catches Mom's eye in the mirror and nods ever so slightly.

Mom's eyes dart back up to the rearview mirror and catch my gaze for just a second. My own tiger eyes—identical versions of hers, with the golden sparkle, the flecks of green, the rim of brown—try to tell her what I'm feeling. They try to explain about the monster under the lake.

"I'll be late to the General Store today, maybe four thirty. I told Mrs. Grant, and she said that was fine. Will you be okay?"

I nod. Taylor's grandma has been giving me extra cheese on my grilled cheeses at the General Store soda fountain for three full years now. She makes me milk shakes and lets me pick out a handful of penny candy anytime I want. It sounds amazing, like a birthday wish come true. But I'd trade all the cheese in the world to have Clara back.

Even now. Even when it's not supposed to hurt every single day.

My eyes brim with tears but the annoyance of almost crying, *again*, seems to shut them down, thankfully. Taylor reaches over and squeezes my hand really quick.

Old Betsy grunts and wheezes her way around the rotary in the center of town. Instead of a stoplight, there's a huge fountain in the middle of the road that everyone has to drive around. A lot of days I think I feel like the fountain must feel. Everyone staring at it, wondering why it doesn't work. It looks totally fine on the outside, maybe a few cracks but nothing that's a big deal. But on the inside, something is definitely wrong. No matter how many experts and repairmen the town hires, no one can figure out why the fountain won't spray water anymore. It's been broken for thirty years because of some dumb prank, and it's like the prank just broke the fountain's heart.

My heart understands. Except that instead of NOT being able to spew water into the sky, I can't seem to stop spewing water from my eyes. None of the experts can fix me either. And believe me, a lot have tried.

Mom steers Old Betsy into the school drop-off lane and I thank the Universe that my water-spewing eyes seem dry right now. My heart is about to explode, but that I can handle.

That no one can see.

"Have a good day, sweetie," Mom says as Taylor shoves open the heavy car door and jumps to the curb.

You know those videos that are speeded up super fast? The ones showing a leaf falling from a tree, drying up, curling, and turning to dust in a matter of seconds? That's how I feel when Mom calls anyone—especially Taylor—"sweetie." But these days, pretty much anything that comes out of Mom's mouth makes me want to either crawl in a hole or run away as fast as I can (which is not very fast, but still). I can't exactly figure out why anything she does makes me want to leap out of my skin, but there you go.

Just another unfortunate mystery orbiting Amelia Peabody.

I kick open the car door and grab my nearly empty messenger bag.

"I love you!" Mom calls after me.

I want to call over my shoulder, "I love you, too!" but I don't. I mean, as far as last words go, *I love you* is pretty good. Yet . . . there's this part of me, a huge part, that wants to believe I can keep her safe by not saying anything at all. You can't get into a fiery car crash, you can't get struck by lightning, you can't trip and fall and break your neck, you can't be swallowed by the lake, if there are no last words. Right?

Taylor and I walk toward the big live oak tree in front of the school. I don't look back at Mom, even though I hear Old Betsy wheezing, even though I hear the car behind her gently honking. I hold my hand up over my head, a wave, even though I don't turn around. And finally, Old Betsy harrumphs out of the drop-off line and Mom is safe.

"Who run the world?" Taylor knocks her shoulder into mine and grins.

"Girls!" I grin back.

The bell rings and we both take a deep breath. We link arms and walk up the stairs through the heavy doors. My chin is high, but my heart is pounding. I try to ignore it. Usually all eyes are on me because I'm the poor girl with the dead sister. But now all eyes are on me because I WANT all eyes on me. No one feels sorry for Sandy in *Grease*. No one feels sorry for Beyoncé. Surely, my face only looks pale because of the tight black T-shirt. Definitely not because I'm afraid someone will call my bluff and realize I'm still the girl with the dead sister, the one who can't be trusted to speak out loud in class because she might burst into tears.

No. I'm the new Amelia. They're staring at me because they know I mean business. They know eighth grade is mine for the taking.

Well, mine for the taking after I peel my face from the edge of the doorway.

"Amelia!" Taylor's hands are over her mouth as she does a poor job of stifling her laughter. "Um. Watch out."

Perfect. Arriving in homeroom with a crease down the middle of my forehead was exactly what I had planned. Sigh.

Instead of milling around and talking about summer vacation, everyone in the classroom wanders from desk to desk scanning papers, with shrieks and moans and laughs filling the room.

"Wha—" I look to Mrs. Henderson, our new home-room teacher. *New* meaning for eighth grade. Mrs. Henderson herself has been on the earth since the asteroid killed the dinosaurs.

"On each desk is a letter. Remember the ones Mrs. Werther had you write on your first day of sixth grade? Well, now it's time to find your letter and see what you've accomplished."

Mrs. Werther is even older than Mrs. Henderson. She was one of the aliens that rode in on the asteroid.

Taylor and I start to scan the desks, too. Taylor calls out, "Found mine!" and she sinks into her chair look-ing like she's ready to burst into terrified laughter. I walk up and down each aisle, not finding my name. The late bell echoes through the room and Mrs. Hen-derson shuts the classroom door. I'm starting to freak out. Where's my letter?

A desk toward the back of the classroom is empty, so I hurry over there. Surely, that has to be mine.

Dear Most Beautiful Queen of the Universe (snort).

I suck in my breath, running my hands over the impressions made by the pen and smoothing the letter flat on the desk.

NO.

No way.

Dear Self,

You have made it to sixth grade, no thanks to that seriously goofy little sister of yours and her obsession with trying to steal clothes from your closet. Hello, scaring me to death this morning when all I wanted was a clean shirt. GAH!

Holy Beyoncé. This is Clara's letter!

Without realizing what I'm doing, I drop into the chair attached to the desk. I hold up the letter and it shakes in my hands like my body thinks it's made of plutonium.

Mrs. Werther said to write something to yourself that would be inspiring when you read it on the first day of eighth grade. So. Hmm.

How about: Congratulations on making all your dreams come true! Making some of your dreams come true? Making at least a couple of them true? Remembering to just dream in the first place?

Well, in case you haven't made all of your dreams come true, here are some things I really hope you HAVE accomplished. And if you haven't... get after it, girl. Next year is high school! OMG.

1) Be nicer to Mom and Amelia. (Why is it easier to be nice to Dad? Try to not let

Mom and Amelia annoy you so much.
Remember, you love them. So much.)
2) Get on the softball team. (You're good.
Everyone says you're good. Always
remember... you're good.)
3) Ask Billy to a dance. (OMG. Billy. Sigh.)
4) Throw an awesome birthday party on the
lake. (Invite everyone, make sure the boat
is working, have enough ice cream for the
whole town, make sure everyone knows
it's YOU, Most Beautiful Queen of the
Universe, in charge.)
5) Plan the most epic eighth-grade prank ever.
(But do a better job than Dad did for his
prank—don't break the FOUNTAIN. Wow,
Dad, way to take it to the next level.)
  Seems doable, right? I mean, you ARE the
Most Beautiful Queen of the Universe. Anything
can happen.
  Good luck surviving middle school!
Love,
Yourself

I hear Clara's voice as I read the letter over and over.
It's as if she is leaning behind me and whispering in

my ear. Hot, embarrassing tears threaten to overflow down my cheeks.

I'm supposed to be tough and strong this year. How can I be tough and strong with Clara whispering in my ear about all the things she never got to do? And even worse . . . the one thing she did get to do: the birthday party at the lake.

The day the monster awoke. The day that was the end of everything.

"Amelia? Are you okay?" Mrs. Henderson's voice breaks through the clouds and mist of grief, and my head flies up to face my teacher. I grip the plutonium letter and want nothing more than to bolt from my desk, run home, and never come back to school. Ever.

"I'm—I'm fine," I manage to whisper. Taylor shoots me a look from across the room. If you have to say, "I'm fine," usually you are definitely not fine. This is something the two of us discuss a lot.

After an agonizingly slow nine-million-hour homeroom, where all sounds and instructions seem to be coming through a tunnel a million miles away, where my head seems to be floating over my body, where I clutch the plutonium letter to my chest, afraid to breathe too deeply because I might combust into a cloud of atoms, the bell for first period rings. Everyone stumbles out of their desks and moves to the doorway. Taylor is by my side in about 2.7 seconds.

She kneels next to my desk, putting a hand on my arm. "Amelia. What is it?" I can't say anything. I can't move. She gingerly reaches over and pulls the now crumpled letter from my grip. As soon as she reads the top of the page, her hand flies to her mouth. She looks up at me, her eyebrows crinkling in an angry V shape.

"Do you think someone did this on purpose? To upset you? Who would do that?" Her eyes cast around the room, but everyone else is gone.

I like that Taylor always wants to protect me, but I don't think this was some mean trick. "I'm pretty sure Mrs. Henderson just saw the last name and got things mixed up. It's a miracle she's even still teaching. She's got to be at least one hundred and fifty years old. It had to have been an accident."

"Or some kind of divine intervention." Taylor's eyes are huge and her eyebrows now make wide arcs on her forehead. "Maybe this is the Universe's way of telling you you're on the right track—eighth grade really is the time for you to take over the world."

"What do you mean?" I sniff and realize there are tears spilling down my cheeks. That's me now: The Girl Who Doesn't Even Know When She's Crying.

Taylor glances down at the letter and then looks back up at me. "I mean, maybe you can do some of these things Clara has listed. You want to break out of your shell, right? What if you follow her lead?"

I reach over and take the letter from her, running my fingers over the handwriting on the paper. I can see where Clara's pen stopped for a minute while she must have been thinking about what to say next. I can see how her writing got messier when she was excited. I feel the grooves in the paper where she pressed her pen hard, making sure her words hit the page just right. It's like a little piece of her is here with me, after all this time. Something new, things I didn't know about her. Who is Billy? What does she mean about Dad being one of the kids who broke the fountain? I thought I knew everything about her, but here's this sudden peek into a girl I didn't really know.

"That'd be cool, wouldn't it?" Taylor presses. "You showing everyone that you're tough by following Clara's lead? I'd do it with you." Taylor gives me a hopeful smile.

I know it's probably been so hard for her, being friends with the Crying Girl, having to soothe me and help me on the days when everything just seems lost. That's why she's dressed in these ridiculous black clothes with me, why she wants me to see this as a sign—because if I can be normal again, then she can be normal again.

Maybe Clara's ghost is trying to tell me to be a better friend.

I don't know, though. Find this Billy kid and ask him out? Join the softball team? What would Beyoncé do?

"I think this is a terrible idea," I say.

Taylor claps her hands together and grins as she stands up. "We're doing it, then. AWESOME." I shake my head. Taylor is good at a lot of things, but not getting her way isn't one of them. She reaches down and helps me out of my seat. The classroom is filling with students for the next class.

"Come on, we're going to be late." Taylor drags me out into the hallway, pulling my schedule from my backpack, looking at my classes, and steering me toward algebra.

Is this crazy? This is crazy.

I don't actually want anything on Clara's list. If I'm honest with myself, I don't want to be wearing these black clothes. Do I even *want* to be queen of the eighth grade?

I think about my comfy bed. I think about pulling the covers over my head and just staying there, forever, like Dad almost did when Clara died.

I trip over my shoelace and Taylor catches me just before I sprawl out in the hallway.

"We might have to brainstorm a little about that softball thing," she says through a laugh.

This really is a terrible idea.

CHAPTER THREE

"EXTRA CHEESE?" MRS. GRANT'S SHARP stare bores holes in me and I wonder what secrets are leaking out.

"Yes, please," I say, looking down at the countertop. There are sparkly green flecks in the Formica. The Grants are very proud that the General Store hasn't been redesigned since it was built by Taylor's great-grandmother way back in the 1950s. It's like walking into a time warp, with the counter area for milk shakes and hamburgers, and the pharmacy in the back. How many places can you go get lunch, candy, toilet paper, and your allergy medicine all at the same time? Not many.

Mrs. Grant is flipping my grilled cheese on the griddle behind the counter. Her silvery hair is bunched up on top of her head, but the swirls of curls refuse to stay tied down and spring out all around her face and neck. I don't know how old she is, but she's never seemed like a grandma to me. She doesn't say a lot, but her eyes are these, like, magical black orbs that can apparently see into people's souls. Folks will sit at the counter and spill all their problems and ailments, and Mrs. Grant will listen intently and then offer a sandwich or a milk shake or a steaming order of hand-cut fries that seem to miraculously solve everyone's problems. At least for a few minutes.

I have more than a few minutes today, with Mom running late. I have no idea what her job is now that she's a "part-time city consultant" instead of the city manager, but whatever it is means that she's late a lot, and wears heels a lot. Not much different than before, really, except now when she's late, it means four thirty instead of eight thirty.

Taylor is upstairs in the apartment she lives in with her parents and grandma. She didn't say so, but I could tell she was ready to get out of the all-black clothes and put on one of her summery dresses. Taylor is a huge fan of flowy and flowery. I am so not, but I don't begrudge her. Just like she doesn't begrudge me my Chuck Taylor sneakers and constant stream of beat-up T-shirts.

I think my mom wishes I would dress more like Taylor, more like how Clara dressed, but she never says so out loud (unless you count deep sighs when I come downstairs dressed for the day).

"Let me know what you think." Mrs. Grant flips the grilled cheese onto a plate and pushes it toward me. She pumps a big squirt of vanilla syrup into a glass, scoops in some ice, and fills the rest with Coke from the hose thing connected to the big soda cylinders under the counter. I don't know why Cokes taste so much better here than anywhere else, but boy, do they. She gives the vanilla Coke a spin as she slides it to me, a smile sliding onto her face as well. She wipes her hands on the towel that always hangs from the front pocket on her apron.

"So," she says, her elbows on the counter, and her chin in her hands. "How is eighth grade so far?"

I take a bite of the sandwich and can't help the moan that escapes my lips. I catch a string of melted cheese dangling from my chin. "What is that? Cheddar, Havarti, and . . . did you put a sour apple in this?"

Mrs. Grant's eyes twinkle. "You're avoiding my question," she says. "Tell me about your first day." She winks and whispers, "Just a couple of thin slices of a Granny Smith apple. I know how you feel about tart things. If you like it, I'll make it a daily special and you can help me name it."

Naming the daily specials is a fun exercise in just the right puns. Taylor is really good at coming up with great ones. *Don't Go Bacon My Heart* was one of her best (BLT with extra B). And *Another One Bites the*

Crust was her idea for the French toast special. My suggestions are getting better. *I'm Kind of a Big Dill* tuna salad is one I'm proud of.

I take another bite and talk around the slight crunch. "It was mostly okay." I think about the letter, and about not saying anything about it. But there's something about those piercing eyes. They reach inside of me and I can't help but spill.

Taylor walks through the curtain in the back that hides the stairs leading up to the apartment. Her dog, Ratface, is right at her feet, hopping around like a squirrel. I'm not sure you're supposed to have a dog in a general store, but no one has ever said anything. Ratface is basically an unpaid employee. His job is to make everyone laugh. Taylor sits beside me and steals a fry just as I'm finishing up the story about Clara's mystery letter.

"She's going to do the things on Clara's list," Taylor says, nudging me with her shoulder and then dropping a fry to Ratface, who gobbles it up in one snap of his tiny jaws.

I give her a weak smile and feel Mrs. Grant's stare laser its way into my brain. "*Are* you going to do that?" Mrs. Grant wipes the countertop as she looks at me. I look up at her and then at Taylor. Taylor's smile is so wide I wonder how it's possible. Could my face even stretch like that anymore?

"I mean, if I'm going to take eighth grade by storm, maybe it would help with that?" I eat a fry and it suddenly has no taste.

"But, Amelia, honey, do you *want* to take eighth grade by storm?" Mrs. Grant sets her towel off to the side and puts her hand on my hand. For some reason, this makes me want to just cry and cry and cry. Because honestly? I don't know what I want. I just don't want to feel like this anymore.

I shrug. "At least it would be different."

"Different how?" Mrs. Grant is very good at asking questions, her voice so soft it's like the opposite of her eyes.

I shrug again. "Doing something would be a nice change. Does that make any sense? Like . . . I can't talk to Clara anymore. She can't roll her eyes at me. She can't be grouchy with me for borrowing a shirt. But crying all the time doesn't accomplish much, does it? It doesn't bring her back, and it doesn't make me miss her less." I choke back a knot in my throat. "So maybe I could get closer to her by trying to figure out why these things were so important to her? I don't know. It sounds stupid when I say it out loud."

Mrs. Grant and Taylor both stare at me. This is maybe the longest string of words I've strung together in about three years.

"Wow. You've been thinking a LOT about this."

Taylor's eyes are wide. Mrs. Grant's hand is still on mine.

"What does your heart tell you to do?" Mrs. Grant squeezes my hand.

"My heart tells me it doesn't want to hurt so much anymore." I look down at my half-eaten grilled cheese, the swirling tears in my eyes blurring it into a big blob.

"You're going to have to go to all the parties with me," I say, my voice thick with unshed tears. I clear my throat. "And help me figure out who the heck Billy is."

"Of course, of course! It's going to be fun, Amelia!"

I swipe at my eyes and notice the fountain through the front window. Some little kids are trying to climb the giant bird in the middle of the fountain. The bird stuck in stone forever. I don't want to be stuck in stone forever. Even if it's easier that way.

CHAPTER FOUR

"HEYA, KIDDO!" DAD GRABS ME up in a hug as soon as Mom and I walk in the door. Mom drops her keys on the kitchen counter and her bag on the floor. She looks like she's had a rough day. Is it possible for grown-ups to even *have* as rough a day as the first day of eighth grade? I thought the whole point of her doing this part-time consultant thing was to have *less* stress and *more* time at home. I think maybe she's doing it wrong.

"Did you ruin your appetite?" Dad smells like meat and barbecue smoke, his big hairy arms tickling my less hairy arms as he holds on tight. I don't say anything because I know he'll keep talking. Dad isn't big on silences. "You think you might want to try out some new sauces? I've been experimenting."

"Uh-oh." Mom cracks open a soda and tries to crack a smile, too. "More experimenting?"

Peabody's Pits 'n' Pieces is Dad's new adventure. He's always loved to cook on the grill. And he's always loved meat. So, after he went crazy a while back and quit his job as a computer programmer and spent like three months in bed, he finally decided he was going to start a barbecue restaurant.

I could tell Mom thought he was nuts. Those golden eyes of hers can't hide her feelings very well. But just like he didn't say anything when she spontaneously quit her job so she could "enjoy more family time" and then just as spontaneously asked for half her job back so she could "feel useful," *she* didn't say anything when he came back from the bank in his rumpled funeral suit with a grin on his face. She also didn't say anything when he went on and on about barbecue smokers and different kinds of wood and spice rubs. She didn't even say anything when he decided he'd rather have a food trailer than an actual restaurant, and parked a sleek silver bullet Airstream in our front yard until the neighborhood snobs made him move it. It's been a couple of years since Dad found his voice again (and Mom started working fake part-time), and since then, there has been a LOT of experimenting and tasting and talking about barbecue.

I don't really mind. The more he talks, the less I have to. And the more Mom is at work, the more Dad and I get to hang out. Plus, I like meat, too.

Now Dad takes my bag and herds me and Mom into the kitchen. There are little glass dishes all over the counter, filled with mystery sauces. There's also a slab of smoked, but sauceless, spare ribs. Dad drops my bag by the table, throws on his apron, and starts whacking at the ribs with a cleaver. He doesn't really need to whack them, though. The meat falls right off the bone.

His voice is soft as he says, "There's gonna be a cook-off at the lake later this month. Food TV people are going to be there. It could be huge for Pits 'n' Pieces. What do you both think about going? Cheer me on? Maybe get to make a silly face on national TV?"

Mom says nothing. I say nothing. I'm going to pretend I didn't hear him over the tsunami of saliva in my mouth. Not a lot of things make me legitimately happy these days, but a mouthful of rib meat dissolving on my tongue comes pretty darn close, even if my belly is full of fries and a grilled cheese.

I will not let a mention of the lake ruin that.

Dad clears his throat and starts pointing at the dishes of sauce. "I have spicy and mild. Sweet and tangy. And this one . . ." He gestures proudly. "I might have to make you sign a waiver before you try it. Ghost peppers." He waggles his eyebrows and makes a *whoosh* noise like a firework shooting into the sky.

Mom and I dig in while Dad watches with a look on his face that is both proud and terrified. He's like a kid at the science fair. Will the judges give him a blue ribbon? Or are his experiments too strange?

I point at the one that is suspiciously orange. "I like to eat this one, but I don't like to look at it." Dad nods and pulls a little notepad from his apron pocket. He jots something down and sticks the pad back in his pocket. "Noted," he says with a grin.

Mom points to the ghost pepper one, tears streaming down her face, sweat beading on her upper lip. "Wh-where's the waiver?" she stammers. I can't help but laugh.

"So, tell me about your first day of eighth grade, Amelia!" And just like that, Dad kills the mood. Suddenly, the sauce in his beard doesn't seem charming anymore. It is annoying.

Why can't he just let us have five seconds to live in a moment? All of a sudden, I feel like I might cry. I swallow around the growing lump in my throat and put down my rib bone. I lick my fingers as I blink back tears and shrug. "Fine?"

"A truer answer has never been spoken." Dad gives me the tiniest of sideways looks and then starts tossing the little dishes in the sink. "At least you have the big prank this year. That's something to look forward to, yeah?"

"Oh, Jim, don't start." Mom can't help but smile, though. He's still at the sink and she slides behind him, her arms around his big belly. They are so gross. I mean, come on. They were in eighth grade together. Heck, they were in kindergarten together. This town is like the La Brea Tar Pits, collecting souls, no escape.

For years my textbooks have had Mom's or Dad's name in them. (Small-town school funding, yikes.) Sometimes I've even had the same *teachers* they did. It's insane. So, yes, I know Mom's prank was yarn bombing a bunch of light poles on Main Street. Dad's prank was huge and had something to do with stop signs and getting in trouble for endangering the public. Or at least that's what I was always told. My hand clenches around Clara's letter folded in my pocket.

I have no idea what my prank will be. Like zero idea.

I leave the two of them in the kitchen and take my bag upstairs. Lying on the bed, I stare at the ceiling. There was never really a game plan for what Taylor and I would wear to school on the second day of eighth grade. I get up and open my closet.

There's a knock on my door and Mom sticks her head in. "You going to bed already?"

I don't know. I feel like I can never answer any of her questions. Even the simple ones. I shrug, which has become my signature move.

Mom sneak-attack hugs me before leaving the room. I close my closet door and look at the empty bed on the other side of the room. The quilt is the same. The pillows the same. Mr. Bear leans to the side, his left ear hanging by a thread. I walk over to the other closet, the big one, the one I was never allowed to open.

I open it.

There's a flowy top covered in a bunch of bright colors, and a jean skirt. That was the outfit Clara chose for her first day of eighth grade. The outfit she never got a chance to wear. And in the back, behind another flowery shirt and some white jeans, there's a black shirt with a streak of silver down the side. I take it out of her closet and put it in mine.

CHAPTER FIVE

"OKAY." MY HANDS ARE ON my thighs as I lean over, breathing harder than I have possibly ever breathed. "I—it's—can we stop now?"

Taylor jogs in place next to me. "Stop?!" She looks like I just told her Beyoncé is retiring. "We've only run half a mile. HALF a mile, Amelia! That's basically nothing."

"I might puke," I say to the ground, swallowing hard, my heart still pounding.

"You're not going to puke. After mile five, you can puke. Come on. Let's go!" She grabs my arm and gently pulls. I plant my feet and not so gently pull back. She stumbles toward me.

"Hey, hey, heeeeeeey!" A tall boy on a skateboard whooshes past, flips the board on its end, turns, and comes back toward us. He's wearing a helmet that looks like a shark is eating his head.

"Hi, Twitch," I breathe. "What's the story?"

"Same as always," he says, skating circles around us. "Though you freaked me out for a minute, out here in those sporty clothes doing sporty things. Thought for a second the ghost of Clara was haunting me." His lopsided grin doesn't match his sad eyes. Twitch and I used to see each other every day. He hung around Clara like a lost puppy, and she tolerated him because . . . well, I don't really know why. I guess because she could boss him around and he would do anything for her. It's hard for me now, to see him around. When he appears, it's like the world goes foggy and I zoom through some kind of time warp. I can only ever see him, soaking wet, running in from the lake, arms waving over his head, screaming her name in a voice I'd never heard before, or heard since. The kind of terror and panic he must have been feeling, it made his voice jagged, louder than possible, high-pitched. You could almost see the spiky words shooting from his mouth: *Help! Clara! Underwater! Boat flipped! Help! Help!*

I stand up straighter, taking my hands off my thighs, my posture suddenly reminding me of Twitch catching his breath as the grown-ups ran past him to a motorboat and then sped to the middle of the lake.

Can you be in love with someone when you're in the sixth grade? I don't know. But maybe Twitch was in love with Clara. I don't think she was in love with him, though. Maybe that's the saddest thing of all.

"Whatcha doing?" he asks, turning tighter and tighter circles. The silver bracelet he always wears glints in the sun and blinds me for a second. You'd think a sophomore in high school wouldn't care what little eighth graders were up to, but you'd be wrong. We have a weird connection, Twitch and I. When you've stood next to someone and breathlessly watched the world end, it gives you a bond whether you want one or not. That sounds dramatic, but it's true.

"Amelia is broadening her horizons," Taylor says, switching from jogging in place to jumping jacks. "She is endeavoring to break out of her shell."

"'*Endeavoring*'? You sound like my mom."

"I'm just saying you're attempting something big. Big things need big words."

I feel my eyes start to roll, but I try to stop them. I don't want to be grouchy with Taylor. She's trying to help. And I know I need help. I mean, I guess I do. Moping for three years? A huge cry for help, right?

"How is puking in the street broadening your horizons?" Twitch's eyes finally match his smile.

"I am not puking!" I put my hands on my hips. "At least not yet. Anyway, I'm doing it for Clara." I reach into the tiny zipper pocket in the back of my running shorts and pull out her letter, where I stashed it, folded as tightly as possible. It's a little damp from my sweat, but not enough to smear the ink, just enough to make it kind of limp in my hand. I hand it to Twitch.

"I'm going to make sure everything on her list gets taken care of."

He takes it, barely pinching it between two fingers.

"It's not covered in poison, dork, just my sweat."

"Why would I take your word on that? How do I know you aren't some kind of mutant? The risk seems high." Twitch is trying to hold the limp page in a readable position. He has to stop skating and arc his head toward the sun as his two fingers dangle the sweaty paper in front of his face.

I watch him read it, his face going from that smirking-joking-Twitch-expression to solid stone. The pink in his cheeks goes pale. When he's finished, he carefully folds the paper, following the creases that are already there. He hands it back to me. I don't think he cares about the sweatiness anymore.

"You're going to do all these things?" His voice is a little rough. He clears his throat and looks down at his board.

I feel my infuriating tears threatening once again and nod. "It's not like I'm trying to BE her, or anything. It just seems like I can help her do the things she didn't get to do, and she can help me . . ." I can't think of what to say. Be happy? Stop feeling terrible all the time? I don't want to say any of these things out loud.

Twitch's dark brown eyes gaze off into space. "Yeah" is all he says. After a minute where we're all kind of quiet and lost in our own thoughts, he smacks his foot on his skateboard and says, "Well, you lovely young women, have a wonderful day," and he's off down the hill, out of sight.

"Oh, Twitch," Taylor says softly. Then she looks at me, her eyes bright, her mouth doing a frown-smile thing. She looks so much like a grown-up sometimes.

"Come on, let's take a break."

"Milk shakes?"

"What else?" Taylor links her arm in mine and we head toward the General Store.

CHAPTER SIX

"I AM THE DRAGON BREATHING fire! Beautiful mane, I'm the lion!" I hold my spoon like a microphone and screech into it, eyes screwed shut, feeling the music snake its way into my body, making me move in a way I couldn't without the beat and the flow and . . . Man, I love music.

"Settle down, settle down. Your Beyoncé karaoke is going to scare away all my customers." Mrs. Grant jogs down the stairs and turns off the radio Taylor and I have cranked up loud. She looks at us with this expression of amusement and grouchiness, but also maybe fondness? Maybe?

"You knew that was Beyoncé?"

"Everyone within a twenty-mile radius knows that was Beyoncé, Amelia."

Taylor licks her spoon and points it at me. "She's right. Please don't make the whole town go deaf."

I roll my eyes, but in a joking way. Nothing like a milk shake and Beyoncé to cheer me up. Except . . . the ding-ding of the front door echoes through the store and, yep, it's Mom. Right on time. Ratface runs over to her to say hello. She leans over and pats him on the head, but even his cute lolling tongue can't stop my good mood from leaking into the air like helium escaping from a balloon.

"Everyone having fun?"

Why do moms have to say such dumb things? I can't even answer her. For some reason, though, Mrs. Grant and Taylor don't seem to think it's ridiculous and they babble on about how we're fine and how I'm going to be in great shape soon. Mom's face squinches in that way it does when she's confused. I do a zip-it motion with my hand, and Taylor's eyes go wide. Thank goodness for best friend mind-reading abilities.

Mom doesn't know about the letter.

"And here I thought it was strange that you woke up so early to meet Taylor. Now I find out you woke up early to go *running*? Who *are* you?" Mom's tone is light but those tiger eyes tell me she's weirded out.

"Just trying to get that mind-body thing going," Taylor says, her smile so big that it might blind us all. "Did you know that exercise can help depression?"

Mom turns to me and I watch her expression go

from weirded out to concerned. "You're depressed, Amelia?" Oh, good grief.

Taylor mouths "Sorry!" over Mom's shoulder. Only I can see her, and I try not to glare. This hole is getting deeper and deeper.

"Can we just go?" I pop my earbuds in, letting the music drown everyone out. I see their mouths moving, and I choose not to figure out what they're saying. I hope "Can we just go?" is not the last phrase I ever say to my mother, but right now, I want out of here and for her to stop talking and just . . . to find a hot shower. Is there any possibility I'll be in shape enough to try out for softball in four months? Do I even care?

I wave at Taylor and walk out of the General Store. I climb into Old Betsy, the cracked vinyl seat snagging at my running pants. I feel like everything is snagging at me these days. It's never enough to tear a hole, only enough to annoy me.

I wonder if Clara ever felt like Mom wouldn't give her enough space. She did put the thing on the list about being nicer to Mom. I think about how she used to mimic Mom when she was mad, using this ridiculous singsong voice. It always made me laugh, even when steam would shoot from Mom's ears.

To me, Clara always seemed like she had everything figured out. She knew what she wanted and went for it. But maybe she had doubts, too. Hmm. I pull the now-dry letter from my pocket and read over the list for the thousandth time. Maybe she didn't always go for it. Maybe Clara was an illusion like the rest of us.

"What do you have there?" Mom asks, her eyes meeting mine in the rearview mirror.

I carefully fold up the letter and shove it under my butt. "Nothing!"

Mom blinks at me and then her eyes are back on the road.

Sigh. Excellent work, there, Amelia. THAT wasn't suspicious at all.

"So, you know how I was late picking you up yesterday?" Mom navigates around the fountain, and I imagine what it must have looked like full of water sparkling from the sun. I bet it was loud, too, with all the rushing water. It must have been nice to sit on the edge and feel little splashes in the hot sun.

"Amelia?"

I snap back to attention. "Uh. Right. Yes. You were late yesterday."

"I was late because I finally had that meeting with Mr. Robertson. Remember the one I set up last year when school was almost out for the summer?"

My brain tendrils reach back into the recesses of my mind. I can feel the memory surfacing. Then it crashes through my body with an electric jolt. "Yes! About my possibly testing out of eighth-grade science and taking physics this year?" I had forgotten all about that! My body zings at the thought of escaping earth science and getting my hands dirty in the high-school physics lab.

"Well," Mom says as if she's a magician about to reveal a cornucopia of delights inside a previously empty box, "Mr. Robertson said you can come by the high school and take a physics benchmark test. You'll also have to take the eighth-grade earth science final exam to prove you know the material and will be fine skipping the class. Pass both of those and you're in."

I let her words fly around in my head as we drive by the lake. I listen to the monster under the water growl low and mean. Clara never got the chance to take earth science or physics. Well. I'll ace them both for her.

"Can I take *both* tests? Tomorrow?" I ask.

"Both? Tomorrow?" Mom's golden eyes dart back up to the rearview mirror. She catches my gaze and sees I'm serious. "That's not a lot of time to study," she says, but her voice fades halfway through her statement and she smiles. She knows I can do it. I'm not worried at all about taking two tests in one afternoon. I'm also not worried about having barely any time to study for either one. I'm only worried about Mr. Robertson, because I am about to come in and OWN that physics class.

I feel something weird happening to my face.

My cheeks are warming.

My lips stretch out a little bit.

Am I actually smiling? When was the last time *that* happened?

CHAPTER SEVEN

I PUT BOTH TESTS FACEDOWN on Mr. Robertson's desk.

"Done already?"

"Done already." I can feel another smile threatening.

"Well, okay, then." He stands up behind his desk and offers his hand for me to shake. It feels silly shaking it, because I've known Mr. Robertson since I was a baby. I've jumped in piles of leaves in his backyard. I've babysat his dog while he was on vacation. My parents bought our house from his mother before I was even born. It's a *very* small town. "I'll grade these and get back to you."

"How long do you think it will take?" I ask, eyeing the tests, and then his face. I like that he has these black freckles that mix in with his dark skin. I also like how his mustache sometimes hides his expression. I'm always trying to figure out his mood. He's good at being calm and collected, but more often than not, there's a little spark in his eye like a faraway star shining through a dark nebula.

"I think it will take me however long it takes me," he says, and I groan. That makes him laugh. "It won't be weeks, Amelia. I won't keep you in suspense any longer than I have to."

"Thanks, Mr. Robertson," I say. "I can't wait to start class."

"So bold," he says. "So confident." He winks and laughs. I can't help but smile as I walk out of the classroom—and directly into a person walking by.

Oof. The kid's books go everywhere. It's like a ream of paper exploded as we both go sprawling. I'm on the floor, dazed, when I hear a familiar laugh.

"You sure go out of your way to say hello, don't you?" It's Twitch.

"Oh my gosh, Twitch, I'm so sorry!" I quickly stand up and start gathering papers and handing them to him in big unorganized clumps. "What is all of this?" I'm not sure I've seen so much paper in my life. For a second I think I see Clara's name, but then it's lost in the pile.

"Just a project I'm working on," he says as he gathers up papers, too.

We pile all the pages together and he asks, "So what are you doing here, anyway? Not a lot of eighth-grade classes at the high school."

"Oh, I was just visiting Mr. Robertson," I say. I'm not sure why I don't want to tell him about the physics test. Maybe I don't want to jinx it. "He's my neighbor, you know? I, uh, watch his dog sometimes? So, I was . . ." I trail off on purpose, hoping Twitch will interrupt. He doesn't, so we both just stand there feeling weird. Or at least I feel weird enough for the both of us.

"Okay, well, I need to get going," I say.

Twitch smiles. "Nice *running* into you."

"Hey," I say over my shoulder. "I hardly recognized you without your helmet."

He smiles and tries to wave, even though he has about eleven million loose papers in his arms.

I wave and then run out of the building, making sure I don't mow down anyone else. Once outside, I look at my phone. Mom has a city council meeting tonight, and Dad is probably at the barbecue trailer getting ready for the dinner rush. I could either hang out here and wait for Mom to eventually pick me up, or walk over to Grant's General Store and call her from there. It's not *that* long of a walk. And I *am* still trying to get in shape for softball tryouts . . . I hike my backpack over my shoulder and set off.

Walking through town is kind of like walking through a good friend. That sounds weird and possibly gross or ghosty, but I don't mean it like that. I just mean no one is a stranger. Every storefront is familiar. People wave and yell hello from across the street. It's weird to me how I can know pretty much everyone in this place and yet still feel alone most of the time. With Clara I never felt alone. I felt irritated or annoyed. I felt like I couldn't breathe without being compared to her in some way, but when I compare that to how I feel now, I'd take it any day.

When I walk through the door at Grant's, the special is the *We're Gouda Together* grilled cheese. (Gouda and mild cheddar with a smidge of mustard.) Yum.

"How'd it go?" Taylor is behind the counter refilling ketchup bottles. Her apron looks like she's just murdered someone.

"Messy much?" I ask, and she looks down.

"Don't worry," she says, and laughs. "He didn't put up much of a fight."

"I think it went great," I say. "Knock on wood." We both rap our knuckles on the counter, even though it's Formica. "Mr. Robertson has to grade both the tests, and then he'll let me know. He promised not to torture me for too long."

"Ooh! Speaking of torture . . . I think we should add another half mile to our run tomorrow morning. What do you say?"

"I say, I'm going to put up more of a fight than the guy you killed earlier."

"Oh, come on," she says. "A half mile is nothing. You need to build your stamina. Maybe I'll let you speedwalk part of the way."

I look at her with some skepticism.

"I will!" She laughs.

Mrs. Grant walks behind the counter and says hello. I say hello back while I ponder this new half mile.

"Maybe," I say.

"Maybe counts as yes!" Taylor yells over her shoulder as she brings all the ketchup bottles to the storage closet.

"Can I get you a special, Amelia?" Mrs. Grant asks. She's already buttering the griddle, because she knows I could never say no to a *We're Gouda Together*.

"Yes, please," I say. And in a flash, I'm eating a hot, gooey grilled cheese like it might be my last meal. I think about last meals almost as much as I think of last words. I don't care if cheese replaces all vegetables in my life, I'm never eating anything that isn't worthy of a last meal, ever again.

"Have you figured out your prank yet?" Mrs. Grant asks, elbows on the counter, chin in her hands.

"I have not," I answer with my mouth full. "I want it to be something good, and I can't think of anything good."

"You will," she says with a smile. "I have no doubt."

"What about me?" Taylor asks, emerging from the storage closet. "Do you have your doubts about me?"

"Only when it comes to successfully filling ketchup bottles, my dear," Mrs. Grant says. She makes a "gimme" motion with her hand and Taylor strips off her apron. Mrs. Grant throws it in a basket of other dirty aprons and motions for Taylor to go sit beside me. She does, and I begrudgingly give her a bite of my sandwich.

"You know," Taylor says, swiping cheese off her chin, "we could do the best prank together. Come up with something doubly great, but only have to do half the work." She waggles her eyebrows. It's definitely a tempting solution. Plus, it would be fun to work on the prank with her. I don't even know why it's such a big deal. You'd think a town wouldn't want to encourage a bunch of eighth graders to run amok with practical jokes, but maybe by encouraging us to do them all at once, it kind of contains the trouble? Who knows. All I do know is that we have months to plan something before we blow everyone's socks off. That's plenty of time.

The bell on the door dings, and without even turning around, I know it's Mom.

"So?"

Yep. Mom. I turn and feel immediately annoyed at the cheerful inflection of her question. Why so annoyed so fast? How does that happen? What is the science behind this?

I feel myself go stone-faced. "It was fine," I say.

"That's it? Fine?" Mom is standing behind me now. She puts her hands on my shoulders. I shrug them off.

"Fine," I say, and I can hear an edge creeping into my voice. "Regular. Normal. Nothing spectacular." I can see her in the mirror behind the bar. She takes a step back from me and exchanges a look with Mrs. Grant. Mom's face seems to say, "Ouch, give me a break." Mrs. Grant's face seems to say, "Uncool, Amelia," and "I'm sorry, Jen," all at the same time. Now I feel like a jerk.

I turn to face Mom. "I just mean . . . it went fine. I think I did well. It wasn't hard, and Mr. Robertson was nice."

Mom licks her lips and says, "Great." Her voice is flat, the spark gone from her eyes. "Finish up so we can get home." She fishes around in her purse for some money to pay for my sandwich, but Mrs. Grant waves her off. The air in the store is suddenly thick with awkwardness. My fault.

I hop off the stool, wave bye to Taylor and Mrs. Grant, and walk out of the store.

CHAPTER EIGHT

"COME ON," TAYLOR SHOUTS, JOGGING backward. She's up at the top of the hill, and I'm at the bottom. I look up at her and imagine all the things I'd rather be doing right now. Going to the dentist, breaking my leg in a freak getting-out-of-bed accident, standing on a planet while its star goes supernova . . .

"AMELIA! Don't stop! What are you doing? Come on! Come on! I believe in you!" She's clapping now, creating a beat for me to run to. Ugh. I hate this so much. Halfway up the hill, I can't run anymore, so I listen to my screaming legs instead of my screaming Taylor, and I walk. When I get to the top, Taylor looks at me as if I've turned into a pile of dog poo. "I cannot believe you just did what I saw you do."

"What? Make it up Deadman's Hill without becoming a dead man myself? That seems impressive to me. I mean, if I were to ask myself—and I did ask myself—'What would Beyoncé do, if she were about to die on a hill?' my answer, and her answer, would be: Do not die on this hill. So, taking THAT into account, I think I did a great job."

Taylor just stares at me.

Her face is getting pinker by the minute and I can tell she's building up a head of steam. Now might be the time to run.

"You know I'm doing this to help you, right? You know I'm setting goals for you so that you can actually achieve something on Clara's list, right?" She crosses her arms over her chest. I look down at my sneakers. "Sometimes you are your own worst enemy, Amelia, I swear!"

I let her words sink in for a minute, even though I don't like them. Am I my own worst enemy? I don't know. I mean, I'm only doing the things on Clara's letter because Taylor seems so sure it will be good for me. I'm only doing this stupid running because Taylor thinks it will help me get on the softball team. Am I my own worst enemy? Or is SHE my enemy? Trying to make me do things that she knows I'll fail? But . . . that doesn't make any sense. She's my best friend. She obviously doesn't want me to fail.

"Hello. Earth to space cadet." Taylor knocks on my forehead like it's a front door. "What's going on in that head of yours?"

"You didn't tell me the extra half mile was going to be up Deadman's Hill." I can't help but sound sullen. I feel sullen.

Taylor throws her arms in the air. "I'm trying to push you, Amelia. I'm trying to get you out of your comfort zone. I'm trying to help you. Can't you see that?"

"I can. I do. I just . . . why can't we go for ice cream and talk about our feelings instead?" I offer a silly smile, but Taylor is having none of it.

"We can't talk about our feelings, Amelia, because YOU WON'T TALK ABOUT YOUR FEELINGS." She storms off.

"Taylor!" I shout after her. "Taylor, wait!" But she doesn't wait. She runs off, and I know there's no way I can catch up to her. Sigh.

I plod along the side of the street, trying to catch my breath, and not even close to catching my racing mind, when I hear the familiar gravel-scattering sound of skateboard wheels behind me. I turn.

"Heya, stranger. What's cookin'?" Twitch asks. The straps of his helmet dangle under his chin like tentacles. "You out running again? Is the world actually ending, or what?"

"Have I mentioned lately how much I hate running? I hate it with the fiery hot intensity of ten thousand suns."

Twitch laughs. It reminds me of the Before Days, when I'd hear him laughing in the game room when he and Clara would hang out with their friends, playing pool or video games. Twitch is like a human time machine. "I'm going to ask you a question," he says. "And I know it's going to sound crazy. You're gonna be like, 'OMG, Twitch, why would you ask such an insane question?!?!' but I'm going to ask it anyway, because I live on the edge." He pauses and takes a deep breath. "Are you ready?" he asks as he exhales and takes another dramatic, deep breath. "Why are you running if you hate it so much?"

I shove his arm and he laughs again. "You know why I'm running. I showed you the letter. I'm going to try out for softball, because Clara never got the chance to."

"But you hate sweating."

"So?"

"You hate sports."

"So?"

"Uh . . ." Twitch looks genuinely confused.

"I'm doing it because Clara wanted it. I'm trying to complete her letter for her. I don't know." I stop walking, turn, and peer up into his scratchy-looking face. "I'm hoping it will make me feel less sad all the time, okay?"

His face is serious now as he nods. "Yeah, okay. I get that."

We walk together in silence for a little bit longer, when he says, "Why don't you come home with me for a second?"

I can't think of how to answer him. Why would I go to his house? Even though we know each other in, like, the deepest, most horrible ways, we also don't know each other *that* well. He was Clara's friend, not mine. It would be strange to go to his house.

He holds up his hand. "I don't mean come over and sit on the couch and hang out. That would be weird."

I nod, feeling a wash of relief.

"I just mean, I'll grab my sisters' gloves and a softball and we can go play catch. Seems like that might be more helpful for tryouts than all this running."

I think about it for a second, and he has a point. "Okay," I say. "Let's play catch."

He smiles, and we pick up the pace. His house is just around the corner.

CHAPTER NINE

"GOOD!" TWITCH SHOUTS AS I actually catch the softball instead of trying to dive away from it. "Keep your eye on the ball. Nice work."

We've been out here for a long time, tossing the ball back and forth. Or really, he tosses it to me, I duck, it rolls away, I chase it, find it, throw it back, rinse, repeat. It's pretty fun, and I think I'm getting in more running than I did when I was actually running.

"When are you going to tell me what you were doing in Mr. Robertson's class?" Twitch asks as he catches my throw. He's still wearing his helmet as if afraid I might bean him on the head. He might be right.

I think about all the paper he was carrying and how maybe I saw Clara's name. If I answer his question, maybe I can ask him one in return. "I was taking a couple of tests to see if I can start taking high-school physics."

His eyebrows shoot up and are almost lost in the shark teeth encircling his helmet. "Cool. When do you find out if you can do it?"

"Not sure," I say, trying really hard to keep my eye on the ball as it hurtles toward me. "Soon, I hope." I catch the ball and continue, "What were all those papers that I made you drop?"

"If you pass the test, how will it work, do you know?" he asks. I can't tell if he didn't hear my question or if he's ignoring it. "Like, will you walk over from the middle school to the high school? Or do some kind of self-paced thing from home?" He catches my throw with ease and tosses it underhand back to me. I like underhand. I can catch those.

"I'm not really sure," I answer. "I think maybe I'll walk over. I've been trying not to jinx it by thinking too far ahead."

"Oh," he says. "Sorry."

"No, no," I say. "That's okay. *You're* not going to jinx it."

"Why wouldn't *I* jinx it?" he asks, pretending like I've hurt his feelings. "I have excellent jinxing powers."

I'm just about to ask him again about the papers when I hear: "Hey, Twitch." Some kid I don't know walks up to us and they do a kind of high five handshake thing. The kid looks at me and back to Twitch. "You babysitting or something?"

I feel my cheeks burn. Does he think I'm ten?

Twitch laughs. "Nah, man. Just hanging out with my friend Amelia. Amelia, this is Knute."

I hold up my hand in a way that I hope says, "It's not really nice to meet you, please go away," but, like, in a polite way.

Knute nods in my direction but is still looking at Twitch. "Some of us are going over to Grant's for a burger. Want to come?"

"Sure," Twitch says. "We're just about done . . . Aren't we, Amelia?"

I'm about to say something like "I guess" when Knute turns and actually looks at me for the first time.

"Amelia?" he says. "Clara's sister?"

I swallow hard and nod.

"I didn't recognize you," he says, walking over to me. I wish he wouldn't come closer. I feel like this is about to be a conversation I don't want to have. "I was at her party. The one where . . ." He stops and looks at the ground. "Anyway, you look different."

"It *has* been three years," I say, casting my eyes around, looking for anyone, anything, to save me from this.

"Man," Knute says. "That day . . . it was really—"

Twitch sees my face and our moment-of-trauma connection lights up. He grabs Knute by the arm and drags him away mid-sentence. "It was great catching up, Amelia," he says to me, interrupting Knute, and making a har-har sound at his bad pun.

"Uh," I stammer. "Yeah, it was nice to see you." And before I can say anything else, he's whisked Knute off in the direction of the General Store, leaving both gloves and the ball on the ground.

I stand there for a minute, not sure what to do or where to go, and then I realize I'm sweaty and hungry, so I take a deep breath, grab the ball and gloves, and head toward home.

"Heeeeeeey, kiddo!" Dad pulls something out of the oven. Something that smells really, really good. "What have you been up to?"

"Just some exercise," I say, going to the fridge and getting some water. "Nothing crazy."

Dad puts the tray on a towel on the counter. "Check it out," he says. "I'm testing out some desserts for the lake contest. I'm meeting the producers of the TV show up there in a little bit and I thought, why not bring them a little treat?"

I pretend he hasn't said anything about the lake (or about potentially bribing the producers of that stupid contest) and peer down at the tray. It smells super good. Like chocolate chip cookies, but with something . . . different added in.

"Can you smell my secret ingredient?" Dad asks,

pulling a cookie off the tray and tossing it from hand to hand so he doesn't burn his fingers.

I sniff the air. "Hmm," I say. "Is it something savory?"

"Ding ding ding!" Dad says with a smile. "But what?"

"Can I taste one?"

He hands over the cookie he's been tossing and I take a huge bite. It's warm and the chocolate is so gooey it gushes over my lip. "Mmmm," I say, my mouth full. "I taste vanilla and cinnamon and dark chocolate and something salty . . ." My eyes go wide. "Is that *bacon*? Dad! Did you put bacon in these cookies?"

He claps his hands. "Ten points to Ravenclaw!" he shouts. "You like?"

I swallow the bite in my mouth and think about it. I actually do like. I like it a lot. "This is weird and delicious, Dad. Nice work!"

"I really only have a few goals in life," Dad says, looking up to the ceiling with reverence. "To be weird, and to make delicious things."

"Well, if that's the case, then your goals are complete," I say, finishing off the cookie. "Yum."

"Think they'll help push me into the winner's circle at the contest?" he asks, eating a cookie of his own.

Man, man, man. I really don't want to talk about the stupid contest. That's going to mean talking about me coming to the contest, which will mean talking about me coming to the lake, and I am never going to the lake again. So.

"Amelia?" Dad's face is hopeful. He has chocolate in his beard.

"I don't think you need anything to push you over the edge, Dad. I mean, you're already in MY winner's circle." I bat my eyes at him and we both laugh.

"What are you two up to?" Mom is standing in the doorway. She's trying to sound playful, but her eyes have no sparkle. I wonder how long she's been listening. I know she hates it when Dad and I are buddy-buddy. She acts like we're leaving her out of some cool kids' club. It's not that at all. It's just that . . . Dad and I seem to get each other. Like, we're on the same wavelength or something. Mom has her own wavelength. Sometimes I think I can hop along for a ride, but other times, it just seems unreachable.

"Try one," Dad says, tossing a cookie to Mom. Dad seems pretty oblivious to the wavelengths.

Mom catches the cookie and takes a bite, nodding as she chews. "Pretty good," she says.

"Pretty good? Pretty good?! These are officially the best cookies ever made! I mean, come on!"

Okay. I take back the part about Dad being oblivious to the wavelengths. Now he's doing the thing where every word and gesture is about ten times too loud and too big because he's trying to make us laugh, and bring us all together in some kind of made-for-TV family bonding moment. Yeah, no thanks. I grab another cookie and shove the whole thing in my mouth at once so I don't have to say anything. Out the kitchen window I see Mr. Robertson and his dog hanging out on his front porch. Hmm. Would it be against some kind of secret rule if I went over there and said hello and asked how the test grading was going? I chew my cookie and ponder my choices. Go out there, ask about the test, have him refuse to tell me, feel embarrassed, learn nothing new. OR have to talk to Mom and Dad about the contest and the lake. Hmm again.

I head upstairs to shower. If he's still on his porch when I'm clean and have possibly eaten one more cookie for courage, I'll go out there.

CHAPTER TEN

"TINY!" I SAY, SQUATTING AND slapping my thighs. Tiny leaps off the porch, his tongue wagging almost as much as his tail. He leaps on me, knocking me backward, and covers my face with slobbery licks.

"Tiny! No!" Mr. Robertson's yell is half-hearted. I'm pretty sure he knows that Tiny is going to do what he wants to do. Humans only serve to get in his way.

I roll over onto my belly to avoid the licks, and push myself up to my knees and then my feet. This is the only way to escape a Tiny lick attack. I learned this years ago when he was a puppy, but still nearly twice my size.

Mr. Robertson is standing next to me now, in the little dip in the grass that separates his house from mine. He's holding Tiny by the collar, but only because Tiny is letting him. If that dog wanted to, he'd be free as a bird.

"I brought you some cookies, but . . ." I hold up the ziplock bag. Inside is a mound of crushed cookies. "Sorry about that."

Mr. Robertson smiles and takes the bag anyway. Tiny is immediately sniffing at it and trying to nip through the plastic to the bacon he knows is in there. Mr. Robertson taps Tiny's nose with one finger. "No. You've already ruined them. I get all the crumbs to myself." Then he turns his attention to me and tilts his head slightly. "You wouldn't be coming over here to pry certain information out of me, would you?"

"Who, me?" I say, feeling my cheeks get warm. "Of course not."

"Good," Mr. Robertson says. "Because it would be against district policy for me to tell you that you aced both tests. I could get in trouble for saying something like that, so I would never say it. I wouldn't tell you that you should prepare to start taking physics at the high school. And I definitely wouldn't give you an extra textbook to look at so that you're caught up with the class when you join us. Nope. Never would say anything like that. You're going to need to wait for the official call from the school counselor."

Wait. What?!

I jump up in the air and squeal, clapping my hands. This makes Tiny jump up and bark. He's not one to miss a celebration of any kind, no matter how spontaneous or short-lived.

Mr. Robertson is pretending to look stern, but his eyes sparkle. "Wait right here," he says. "And don't let Tiny escape."

I nod. Tiny is on his two hind legs, his front paws hanging over my shoulders. I hold him there and we dance for a minute. Turns out Great Danes are very good dance partners.

Mr. Robertson is back outside in a flash and he offers me the textbook as he lures Tiny off my shoulders with a treat. "I'm not telling you to read up to page twenty-five and be prepared for a pop quiz on Friday. I'm not saying anything of the sort."

I try to look stern, too, but I feel my smile peeking around the edges of my face. "Yes, sir," I say. "It's weird how your mouth has been moving and yet I've heard no sounds come out of it."

He nods back and I take the book. We both grin as he pops a pinch of cookie crumbs in his mouth. "Tell your dad these cookies are pretty good, but I think maybe he mistook some bacon for chocolate chips." He winks as I run back to the house.

"How's Mr. Rob—" Mom starts as I run in through the kitchen door. She and Dad are sitting at the table playing gin rummy, because they are apparently ninety-five years old. I move as fast as I can to the stairs and up to my room, hoping they didn't see the textbook in my arms. I know I *should* want to tell them the good news, but for some reason I don't. I just want to sit with it for a little while, feel the goodness inside me, all mine, before someone says something to make it feel either less good or less mine. I shake my head. Do I even make any sense? I have no idea.

In my room, I sit on my bed and open up the textbook. I run my hand over the smooth pages. There are formulas and equations I could stare at all day. I *might* stare at them all day. I look over to Clara's empty bed. "I did it," I whisper, and point to the book. Then I remember that Clara had no idea I would try to get into high-school physics as an eighth grader. She knew I was good at math, but hadn't seen me blow through my science assignments. She never saw me win the science fair.

Already, the excitement I felt a few minutes ago has dimmed, just a little bit.

There's a quiet knock on my door, and then it squeaks open. I scramble to hide the physics book as Dad walks in.

"Want to go for a ride?" He jangles the keys to Old Betsy. "Maybe grab some ice cream?"

I don't really want to go, but I also don't really want to argue about not wanting to go. "Okay," I say. "But let's do more ice cream and less riding around."

Dad smiles. "Deal."

I should've known something was up when Dad shoved a couple of bags into Old Betsy's trunk before we took off, but I was distracted by thoughts of chocolate scoops and sprinkles. So, once we were all in the car and rounding the bend past the lake, I shouldn't have been surprised when Dad turned down the little gravel road to the lake parking lot.

"Um," I say, feeling my heartbeat ratchet up to about 245. "This doesn't look like ice cream."

"Cookies," Dad says. "Producers. Remember?"

Mom stares straight out the windshield, arm stiff on the car door where the window is open. I get the feeling she didn't know about this pit stop either.

Ahead of us, over a grassy area and near the RV hookups, is Pits 'n' Pieces shining in the sunlight. There's a crew setting up a camera, and a woman in a floppy hat waves and walks to the car.

"James." Mom's voice is low.

Dad reaches over and squeezes Mom's shoulder. "It'll be quick," he says. "Just smile for the camera." He opens the car door and shouts a booming "Hellooooo!" at the woman in the hat.

The lake sparkles just like it did on that day. The color of the sky is the same, too. I can't believe he brought us here like this. I can't believe he's smiling and talking to that woman and not feeling like his guts are going to burst into flames.

"Amelia, Jen . . . come meet Stacy, the producer of *Trailer Takeout*," Dad shouts at the car. "Amelia, grab the cookies from the trunk, please."

I feel shaky and blindsided. Mom squares her shoulders and swings the car door open so hard it bounces away from her and then slams shut again. Oh boy, Dad is in for it.

The rest of the next hour goes by in a fog. Along with every question Stacy the Producer asks me, I hear the lake growling in the distance. During every moment the cameraman zooms in on my face, I see Twitch screaming on the shore. Stacy the Producer explains the rules of the show, but I don't hear anything. I only hear Mom's sobs from that day. I only see horror reflected in the sparkles on the lake.

By the time we're all back in the car, I feel like I've run up Deadman's Hill six times. Mom is silent and seething.

"I'm sorry," Dad says as he puts on his seat belt. "But I knew if I asked you both to come with me for the interview, you'd find an excuse not to. Stacy really wanted the whole family for the background coverage. It's good for the show. Plus, I got to give her some of my cookies. This whole thing is for the success of all of us, remember? It could be a really big deal."

For once, Dad's enthusiasm is lost on me. This was not fun. This was not okay. It *wasn't* the whole family.

"Ready for ice cream?" Dad asks, his voice hopeful as he throws Old Betsy in reverse.

"Just take us home," Mom says, and right now her tone suits me just fine.

Dad sighs deeply while he backs out of the parking space. "I'm sorry," he says again. "But look at it this way . . . we all went to the lake, and now we're all going home. Together. Nothing bad happened. I know it wasn't cool of me to ambush you both like that. I do. But look!" He sweeps his arms wide, despite the fact that he's driving, and his right arm ends up in Mom's face. "It's a beautiful day! We're going to be on a TV show where we'll be made famous! And the lake was nothing but scenery. THAT is a successful afternoon, don't you think?"

Neither Mom nor I say anything. Though deep, deep down in the dark caves of my soul, I can kind of, sort of, maybe, possibly, see his point. Maybe.

CHAPTER ELEVEN

I'M EATING SAUSAGE—NOT BREAKFAST sausage, actual mesquite-smoked sausage, with jalapeños in it—when the phone rings.

"I can't believe you can eat that first thing in the morning," Mom says, walking to the phone. I shrug, dunk my sausage into Dad's special vinegar-based barbecue sauce, then wrap the dripping mess in a tortilla. I take a huge bite and feel my mouth water as the sausage and sauce bite back. Another man's football game snack is my delicious breakfast.

Mom's voice is ratcheting up in volume as she says, "Yes," then "Yes!" then "YES!" and I know this must be the school counselor calling about physics. Mom looks at me as I chew my spicy mouthful and she gives me a thumbs-up. I just stare at her while I chew. Sometimes, out of the blue, I get these flashes of her at the funeral. When she was crying so hard her whole body shook in waves, like human earthquakes. She made this animal noise . . . this wailing . . . that still makes the hairs on my arms stand up when I think about it. I look at her on the phone, giving me a thumbs-up, and for some reason, that's what I see. The sausage in my mouth has turned to dust. I look away.

I hear the beep of the phone hanging up, and in a nanosecond, Mom is by my side, breathless. "You did it!" she says. I can hear the smile in her voice, but my brain is still seeing her wailing at the funeral. "They've arranged for you to start this afternoon. Mrs. James will let you out of history ten minutes early so you can walk over to the high school. Go to the front office, check in, and then go to Mr. Robertson's class. You remember where it is, right?"

"The high school?" I ask, playing dumb.

Mom's face darkens. "You aren't happy about this? No excitement?"

Somehow, all of her excitement seems to be stealing mine away. I wonder if Mr. Robertson's physics lectures can explain that to me.

"I remember where the classroom is," I say, wiping my mouth and standing up. "And I am excited. I promise." I try so hard to smile for Mom, but I'm afraid it must look like I'm being electrocuted. She smiles back at me, looking dubious.

"I have to go," I say. "Don't want to be late."

"Don't you want me to drive you?" she asks as I open the kitchen door.

"Nah," I say. "Extra exercise."

She looks at me in this way I can't really describe. Like maybe I've turned into a very disappointing alien. I flee the kitchen. The cool air outside smacks me in the face and I take huge, deep breaths. Is Mom always going to remind me of the funeral? Is everything?

"Heeeeeeey!" Taylor jogs up next to me. She's back to her flowy dresses, just like I'm back to my T-shirts and jeans. So much for our Sandy-taking-over-the-school attire. Taylor links her arm in mine as we walk down the sidewalk. "You coming to the store after school?"

I nod. "I might be a little late, though."

"Okay, cool. I'm going to be late, too. Lacy and Katherine asked if I wanted to hang out after school." Her cheeks flush and she looks at the ground. I think of Lacy and Katherine, the inseparable duo who always seem to be giggling in a corner somewhere. Does Taylor want to be giggling in a corner somewhere instead of hanging out with me? "I mean, you could come, too, if you want . . ." she adds quickly. I can tell by her voice, though, that I wasn't part of the original invitation.

"It's all right," I say. And, truly, it is. As much as it

makes me feel a little itchy to think of Taylor not wanting to hang out with me, I would *much* rather be studying physics than trying to giggle in a corner. I lift my nose in a snooty way, to make Taylor laugh and lighten the awkward mood. "*I'll* be late because I'll be coming from the high school."

"From the—? Oh my gosh! You got into the physics class?" She stops walking and grabs my other arm. "Amelia! That's so awesome!"

I smile. "It is, isn't it?"

She grabs me up in a bone-crushing hug. "Good work, you!"

I can see her eyes drifting off as a million ideas come to her at once. "You'll be like our high-school spy! You can tell me everything that's happening over there. Who are the cool kids? Who are the ones to avoid? What clubs are the best for meeting people? Who are the cutest boys? Lacy and Katherine are going to pass out when I tell them we have a high-school infiltrator on our hands! Amelia! You're like a spy AND an explorer!"

I push her off of me and laugh a little. "No. I'm just a big nerd. But thanks for your confidence." I want to tell her that Lacy and Katherine totally won't care, but it makes me smile that she wants to brag about me. Even if it's because of my access to high-school secrets.

Taylor stares at me like a parent stares at a kid on graduation day. "First this, then you'll get on the softball team. Soon, you'll be asking out boys and hosting parties. My little Amelia is growing up." She pretends to wipe away a tear.

"Oh, good grief," I say. "Not everything is about that stupid letter, you know."

"It's so not stupid!" she retorts. "You're already coming out of your shell! High school, Amelia! OH EM GEE."

I hate it when she says *OMG*.

"This physics thing is totally separate from the letter," I remind her. "Clara didn't even know I was good at science." My voice catches at the end of the sentence. Great. Am I going to cry? It feels like I've avoided that travesty for the past few days. Ugh.

Taylor hears the waver in my voice and she stops talking. We walk through the front doors of school together and say nothing as we head to our lockers. Lacy waves at her from down the hall and she runs over, linking arms with Katherine along the way. I take a deep, wavering breath, push open my locker, and grab my stuff for first period.

CHAPTER TWELVE

"EVERYONE," MR. ROBERTSON SAYS, HIS deep voice booming through the lab. "This is Amelia Peabody. She'll be joining us for class this semester."

I hear a murmur go around the room, and several instances of people saying, "Peabody?" and "Clara's sister?" and "You remember that girl who . . ." and suddenly the shiny surfaces of the lab tables, the glimmer of the equipment on the shelves, the bright colors of the posters on the walls . . . it all dims. My mouth goes as dry and dusty as the firewood for Dad's barbecue smoker. How did I not predict this would happen? *Of course*, everyone in this class knew Clara. They were all in the same grade.

"Sorry I'm late," comes a voice from the doorway behind me. I turn and look. It's Twitch! He moves past me, drops his backpack on the floor beside a lab table, and pulls up a stool. "Got caught up in art." The glaring eyes painted on the sides of his helmet stare at Mr. Robertson, but Twitch smiles.

Mr. Robertson frowns. "Second tardy this week, Mr. Lewis. You know you only get so many each semester before—"

"I know," Twitch interrupts. "I'm sorry. It won't happen again."

"As I was saying," Mr. Robertson continues while all eyes swivel from Twitch to me, "Ms. Peabody will be joining us this semester. I expect everyone will treat her with just as much—or more—respect than you treat one another." His "or more" was directed at a girl and a boy across the room who were very clearly not paying attention.

"Amelia, you can take that seat there." He points to the stool next to Twitch and I feel a surge of relief. No questions about Clara with Twitch as my lab partner.

"How interesting to see you here," he whispers as we both take out our textbooks.

I smile. "Looks like you just got some hours added to your babysitting job."

He rolls his eyes and stifles a laugh. I'm ready to laugh with him when I see his notebook on the table. In the right-hand corner, scribbled in blue ballpoint pen, it says, "Billy Lewis."

Twitch is Billy?!

Oh em gee.

How did I not know Twitch is Billy? I mean, unless there are two Billys in town? But I'd know if there were two Billys in town. Except . . . there's one Billy in town and I didn't know THAT.

"Amelia? You okay over there?" Twitch looks at me, his forehead wrinkled in concern. I must be hyperventilating or something. The words from Clara's letter bang around in my brain like I'm an unstable atom. "Ask Billy to a dance. (OMG. Billy. Sigh.)"

Clara liked Twitch? How could that be? I remember her bossing him around, teasing him, always challenging him to silly competitions that she knew she'd win. *"Who can eat three Oreos fastest?" "Who can swim to the pier and back first?" "Who looks better in that dumb helmet?"* All of that meant she *liked* him? And now I have to ask Billy to a dance?! He's like seventy-nine years older than I am! Well, three years older than I am, but still.

"Earth to Amelia, psssshhhht, over." Twitch mimes like he's talking into a walkie-talkie, then waves his hand in front of my face. His shiny bracelet catches my eye and snaps me out of my spaciness.

"Huh? Oh, sorry . . ." I stammer. "I just . . . I was . . . what page are we on?"

"Twenty-five," he says, looking at me out of the

sides of his eyes as he bends his head over his textbook.

"Great. Excellent. Perfect," I say as I quickly flip to the right page and thank the Universe that he can't hear my heart beating at supersonic speed.

CHAPTER THIRTEEN

"AMELIA."

"Taylor."

"Amelia."

"Taylor."

I have just told Taylor that Twitch is Billy, and watching her reaction is like watching Ping-Pong balls labeled *O, M,* and *G* fly around behind her eyes. At one point, she lets out a squeal so sharp and loud I'm pretty sure a dolphin somewhere just looked up and said, "Huh. Did someone just call my name?"

"Taylor." I'm trying to keep my voice low and calm.

"Amelia!" Taylor grabs my shoulders and nearly shakes me off my stool. Thank goodness Mrs. Grant is in the storage closet right now, though surely she can hear us. "We are learning so much about Clara. Doesn't this excite you? It's like a new discovery every day!"

"Well, I wouldn't say every day—"

Taylor squeals again. "I love this! Mystery! Intrigue! Amelia, you're like a one-woman reality TV show!"

Mrs. Grant walks out of the closet holding an armful of folded paper napkins. "Who's on a TV show?"

"Amelia!" Taylor shouts with glee. "Well, I mean, she's not. Not yet, anyway. But her life is so exciting, it's like she's on one!"

"Taylor. Good grief. My life is not exciting. It's basically boring with a heaping helping of terrible."

Mrs. Grant gives me some side-eye that looks a lot like the side-eye Twitch gave me in physics. "What's going on?"

Taylor opens her mouth to blurt the whole thing, but I hold up my hand. It's my story. *I'm* going to tell it. "Remember how I'm trying to do all the things on the list my sister made before she . . . before she . . ."

"Yes," Mrs. Grant says, interrupting me so I don't have to say the part I don't want to say.

"Well, one of the things on the list is to ask this boy, Billy, to a dance. He's some guy she really liked, I guess." Then I tell her everything I've just discovered. She points to the chalkboard with the day's special on it. It's the *Romaine Calm*. (Gruyère with butter and crisp, cold romaine lettuce to finish.)

"I'm totally romaining calm!" I shout.

"Yes, I can see that," Mrs. Grant says with a laugh. "Would you like me to make you a sandwich?"

"Do you even have to ask?" I say, running my hands through my hair.

"You know Kite Night is only like a month away," Taylor says, sipping a milk shake.

"I'm not asking Twitch to Kite Night. The dancing is lame. Plus, that's like asking my dad to a dance. If my dad always wore a shark-attack skateboarding helmet and was fourteen feet tall."

"It is not like asking your dad, you goof!" Taylor says, shaking her head. "It's totally not. Look at Beyoncé."

"I love to look at Beyoncé," I say, trying to make it look like I have heart eyes.

"That's not what I'm talking about!" Taylor is getting frustrated with me now, and I like it for some reason. "Twelve years, Amelia. That's how many years separate her and JAY-Z."

"I have to say I'm on Amelia's side in this argument," Mrs. Grant says from the griddle. "Middle schoolers and high schoolers should not date."

"Gram," Taylor says, exasperated. "Amelia is going to be a high schooler next year. Plus, she's practically half a high schooler now."

I'm so tired of talking about this. Sometimes I think if I could just muster half the energy for things that

Taylor can, then I would be so much more . . . I don't know. Just so much *more*. Taylor is like the human equivalent of the word *jazzed*.

My eyes wander to the big window at the front of the store. People walk by quickly and I wonder where they're all going. Probably, they're going home to cook dinner. Or maybe they're going to take their kids to piano lessons. I see moms pushing strollers, and I wonder what the babies are thinking. Are they happy, hungry, sad? Which one of these people walking by will be the lake's next meal? What will be their last words? These babies who haven't even said their first word yet will have last words one day. Hopefully, they'll be old when that happens. But maybe they won't be. What will be the thing they say last? Will it be, "Oh good grief, no you can't come on the boat. You're such a baby." And then will the person answering yell, "I hate you! I hate you! I never want to see you again!" And then will that person always wonder whether she caused the accident to happen with just the will of her voice? Even though she knows that's impossible? Even though a million doctors and therapists and adults have told her it's definitely 150 percent not her fault?

"Amelia. Honey." Mrs. Grant's soft voice makes my eyes move from the window to her face. I didn't even realize I was crying. Taylor is behind the counter now, apron on, not looking at me, wiping down the work surface. Her mouth is open slightly and I can see her poking her tongue at the roof of her mouth, like she wants to say something angry, but is holding back.

Mrs. Grant takes off her apron and comes to my side of the counter. She puts an arm around my shoulder and helps me off the stool like I'm the old lady and she's the Good Samaritan. "Taylor, can you keep an eye on things?"

Taylor nods without even looking up. I wipe the tears off my face and catch some snot with them. Lovely. Mrs. Grant pushes aside the curtains hiding the stairs, and leads me up to their apartment. She throws her hip into the unlocked door and it opens with a bit of a crunch.

"This old building shifts every time it rains," she says. "One day we may not be able to get this door open. We'll have to live in the shop. Which we practically already do." She smiles at me. I can't quite find a smile to give back.

Mrs. Grant leads me into their small living room. I love it in here. It's so worn and comfortable. The Grant family has lived in this apartment since Mrs. Grant was a little girl. You can barely see what color the walls are because there are so many pictures everywhere. And every surface is covered in framed photos and little knickknacks. It's like visiting a very personal museum. I love that you can feel this history in every room. Even the pink bathroom, with the sink that only sometimes works and the tile that's cracked around the bathtub, has this heavy feeling of knowing so many secrets. I like to think that when Mrs. Grant was my age she looked in the mirror in that bathroom and wondered about her future.

"Take a seat, love," Mrs. Grant says. She hands me a tissue and I blow my nose. I feel like such a loser I can't even find the words to apologize. Three years, Amelia, my brain tells me. Three years means you need to stop crying like this. Taylor is right. You have to move on. You are stuck in the mud. I feel the tears well up again as Mrs. Grant brings me some boiling-hot tea and sits next to me on the couch. I can't even sip the tea because it's so hot, but the warmth of the mug feels really good as I hug it with my hands.

Mrs. Grant's hair is especially flyaway today, a tornado of white. She's tried to catch it with a purple scarf, to pull it back in a kind of ponytail, but without much success. She's holding a big old book on her lap. The leather cover is brown, and you can tell that years of being opened and closed, or even just touched, have made the edges a darker brown. She opens the book, and inside there are black-and-white photos stuck to black paper pages. Paper triangles on the corner of each photograph hold them in place. Mrs. Grant carefully slides one of the photos out of its triangles and hands it to me. I put my tea on the coffee table and take the photo.

There are two girls who look younger than me, though not by much. They have their arms around each other and are wearing swimsuits and laughing. The picture is wrinkled, but I recognize the lake behind them. The pattern of the trees on the far shore was the same then as it is now.

"That's me," Mrs. Grant says, pointing to the girl on the left. I hold the picture closer, and even though it's just a smidge blurry I can tell it's her. The crazy hair is a giveaway. "This is my sister, Rosalie." She points to the other girl. The shape of their mouths is the same, but otherwise she looks completely different. She's tall and super skinny, whereas Mrs. Grant was shorter and rounder. Her hair is long and straight, and even though the picture is black-and-white I can tell it was much darker.

"I didn't know you have a sister," I say, looking from the photograph to Mrs. Grant.

Mrs. Grant's face softens. Her eyes close for a second, and then she opens them, but it's like she's looking at something far away. "Rosalie died when she was fourteen," she says.

"What?" My voice comes out a strangled whisper.

"It was an accident." Mrs. Grant's voice is quiet,

but strong. "We were at the lake. I wanted to go out on our canoe, but she didn't want to. She said she was too tired. I was the youngest, though, and used to getting my way. I begged and begged, so she finally said yes. We took the canoe out to a little cove so we could swim, but it was a cove we hadn't been to before. It was closer in, so we wouldn't have as far to paddle back to the shore.

"I was still learning how to dive back then, but Rosalie was one of the best divers in town. She was so tall, and her body bent perfectly when she broke the surface of the water. Anyway, that afternoon, she stood on the tip of the canoe to show me how to dive properly, but what we didn't know was that the water was more shallow than we thought. We didn't know there was a huge boulder just under the surface that we had somehow missed paddling in. She dove in and hit her head."

Mrs. Grant is holding my hand as she tells this story, and I look up at her and see she has tears in her eyes. "I waited for her to surface. It felt like years, eons. Then, when I leaned over the edge of the canoe, I saw her long hair, floating." She stops talking abruptly and puts her hand to her mouth. Then she shakes her head, hard, as if to snap herself out of the memory.

"I'm sorry I never told you about Rosalie until now,

Amelia. I'm terribly, terribly sorry. Taylor doesn't even know about her. She's been my special, painful secret for many years."

My brain is whirling. I can't figure out what to feel or what to say. I vaguely remember, after Clara died, there were some headlines in the paper about the last lake tragedy being fifty years ago, but I didn't pay attention to any of the details. Everything was such a blur.

"I—" I start, but Mrs. Grant interrupts me.

"It's okay, Amelia. You don't have to say anything. I just want you to know that I really, really know how hard this is for you. I know it from the jagged depths of my heart, my dear."

I swallow hard, and my voice comes out a wobbly whisper. "Is it ever going to feel better?"

Mrs. Grant takes the photo from me and lays it on the coffee table next to my untouched tea. She holds both my hands in hers and looks me straight in the eye. "The pain will lessen over time. I promise. But it will always be with you. This grief is part of you now, Amelia. It's the thread that quilts together every other part of your life. I know that right now that must sound terrible to you. And it is terrible, Amelia. It's terrible what happened to Clara. It's terrible that you and your family have had to go through this tragedy. Never let anyone minimize that, okay?"

I nod.

"I can't promise it will get better, but I can promise it will be *different* over time."

I nod again and she wraps me up in a soft, strong hug. "Do you want to see the rest of the pictures?"

I nod for a third time and then we both blow our noses. She opens the photo album and lays it across both our laps as she turns the pages and shows me everything she can about her childhood with her sister.

I don't know how long we've been sitting there when I hear footsteps coming up the stairs. It's Taylor and Mom.

"What in the world are you two doing up here?" Taylor asks. "You're going to get in trouble for violating child labor laws, leaving me down there like that." She laughs and holds up her hand, mimicking the way Mrs. Grant does it. "But don't worry. Mom is down there now so I can get some homework done."

"Time to get home, Amelia," my mom says.

They've both just burst in talking, without even bothering to see what we're doing. Only now do they come over to us.

"What is that?" Taylor asks, looking over my shoulder.

Mrs. Grant closes the album quickly and stands up. "Just some old pictures."

"Ready?" Mom says. "Dad needs our help tonight. He's moving a bunch of equipment to the Airstream," she tells Mrs. Grant. "He's trying to get situated before all the hoopla with that TV show contest."

I give her a look. She was so mad when he tricked us into going to the lake, and now she's going back *voluntarily*?

Mrs. Grant just smiles politely. "See you tomorrow, Amelia?"

I keep looking at Mom, who nods and says, "Is that okay? I feel like I'm taking advantage of your generosity, Mrs. Grant."

"Never," Mrs. Grant says, walking to the door that leads to the staircase. She gives it a yank and it creaks open.

"Don't forget about Kite Night!" Taylor calls after me. I can't read the expression on her face. She doesn't look mad, but she doesn't look super happy either.

Mom shoos me down the stairs before I have a chance to respond. She says good-bye for us both and soon we're out of the apartment, out of the store, and driving away in Old Betsy. As we go past the lake, I hold my breath and stare at its black water in the twilight. It eats every fifty years, huh? Good to know.

CHAPTER FOURTEEN

DAD IS TOSSING SUPPLIES INTO his truck when Mom pulls in the driveway.

"Just in time!" he says with a grin, wiping sweat from his forehead. "I've almost got everything ready and then we can head to the trailer. I want to get it set up and ready for tomorrow."

I feel numb after my talk with Mrs. Grant. I can't catch any of the thoughts flying around in my head except for one: I am not going to the lake.

"Go find some grubby clothes, Amelia," Mom says. "We'll follow Dad over there."

Even if I *wanted* to help empty oil containers and fill sauce containers and stash wood for the smokers (which I don't), I still wouldn't go to the lake. No way.

"I have homework," I say. My voice is monotone

and I don't look back as I push the door open and walk into the kitchen.

"Since when does homework ever take you more than five minutes?" Mom asks, following me inside.

"Since today," I say, walking up the stairs now, still not looking back.

"Come on, Amelia. Get changed. We won't stay for long, just enough to help."

"HOW are you okay with this?" I ask her. "After that ambush?!"

She seems surprised at my bluntness, then she sighs. "Well . . . Dad *asked* this time. And he said he was sorry. This whole thing with the contest and the trailer . . . it's important for the family. Especially with me only working part-time now. We could use the money the show might generate. If he needs our help, we should help."

"Oh, Mom," I say, feeling disgust rise up from my toes. "Way to stand your ground." I shut my bedroom door and push the dresser up against it to prevent any unwanted bedroom breaches that might lead to heartfelt speeches or hugs. Nope. Not going.

It isn't long before I hear a knock. "Amelia. Come on. What's with the attitude?" Mom used to say that to Clara all the time. *"Clara Peabody! What's with the attitude?"* She turns the doorknob, but the door only opens a crack because of the dresser. "What the—" I hear her loud footsteps as she storms off. A minute later, Dad is knocking on the door.

"What gives, Amelia? I'm not loving this behavior. Let's go. Now."

I refuse to say anything. If they can't figure out why I'm so mad, then I'm not explaining it. I don't even know that I could find the words to say if I wanted to say them. Other than *No, Nope, No way, No how, Uh-uh.* Dad sighs deeply and I hear his heavy footsteps go down the stairs. A few minutes later his loud truck engine roars to life. Old Betsy is quiet. Either Mom rode with him in the truck, or she's still here. Doesn't matter. I'm probably not leaving my room ever again.

Lying on my bed, I stare at the ceiling. Mrs. Grant seems like a perfectly normal lady. She always has, ever since I've known her, which has been forever. She's funny and smart and always busy. Everyone in town loves her. It's blowing my mind right now that, even though a horrible thing happened to her sister (a horrible thing she blamed herself for), she's such a . . . regular nice person. She doesn't have a cloud of Dead Sister around her everywhere she goes, like I do. People don't whisper and point at her like they do to me. She goes about her everyday life in a way that seems happy . . . joyful, even. I mean, she whistles and sings to herself, and knows Beyoncé lyrics. HOW IN THE WORLD DOES SHE DO IT?

It's like, for Mrs. Grant, having a dead sister is a thing she keeps inside her, not because she's ashamed of it, or because it's a terrible purple bruise she has to poke, but because, I don't know. Because it's just part of her? Like, Rosalie is alive, but as part of her own soul.

I sit up with a start. How can I make Clara part of me like that?

I hear a commotion out my window that's louder than my racing thoughts. Tiny is barking like crazy, and there's someone shouting. Sliding my curtains to the side, I see Twitch on the sidewalk, holding his skateboard like a shield while Tiny jumps at him and barks. Twitch looks terrified, his helmet all askew, but I can tell by the way Tiny is shaking his booty he's trying to get something. I squint. Yep. There it is. Crumpled up next to the skateboard, gripped hard in Twitch's right hand, is a paper bag from Big Boy Burger, Tiny's favorite. I watch them dance for a second, but it doesn't look like Tiny is giving up anytime soon, and Twitch looks like he might wet his pants. Where is Mr. Robertson?

I push aside my dresser, throw open my door, and run downstairs. It only takes me a couple of seconds to run through the house and get outside.

"Tiny!" I shout, clapping my hands like Mrs. Robertson does. "Cut it out, nerd. You're scaring Twitch!"

Tiny turns to look at me for a split second. He assesses that I don't have a Big Boy burger and he goes back to barking at Twitch.

"TINY!" I shout again, marching up to him and grabbing his collar. "Stop!" He looks at me again and then lunges, licking my face all over. That makes me laugh and splutter. I'm trying to fend him off and signal to Twitch that he's safe.

"Get that burger out of here." I laugh. "You're torturing the dog."

"I'M torturing HIM?" Twitch asks, dropping his skateboard to the sidewalk and holding the burger bag behind his back. "I thought he was going to eat me."

"He just wants your burger. Those are his favorite."

"His fav—" Twitch looks at me, wrinkling his forehead. "You guys are tight, huh?"

Tiny is sitting by my feet now, though he's still nearly as tall as I am. He's happily panting and sniffing around for the burger, giving my face a lick here and there even as I try to shove his enormous head away from me. "We're BFFs for sure," I say. "You okay?"

Twitch gives a sheepish smile. "I'm fine. Maybe my ego is a little scraped up."

"Wait there," I say. "I'll be back in a second."

"Yes, ma'am," Twitch says with a salute. Such a dork.

I hook my finger under Tiny's collar and lead him to Mr. Robertson's backyard. I kick open the fence door and lead Tiny over to the covered porch where I know there will be a bowl of food and water for him. "Here you go, Tiny. It's no Big Boy burger, but it'll do." He gives me a look like, "NOPE," but he doesn't follow me when I go through the gate and shut it behind me.

Back on the sidewalk, I ask Twitch, "Did he jump over the fence?"

Twitch nods, his eyes huge. "It was like some kind of dog-shaped missile heading right at me."

I start to laugh. I can't help it. The image is too funny. Twitch's cheeks turn pink. They're almost the same color as the shark eyes on his helmet. "What are you doing over here, anyway? I never see you skate by."

"Oh," he says, his pink cheeks getting redder. "Actually, there are two burgers in this bag. One for you." He hands me a burger. "You looked a little freaked out in class today, so I thought I'd come by and see if you're okay." He follows me to my front porch, where we sit. "I've discovered that a Big Boy burger can momentarily erase all memories of people in physics classes acting like dummies."

He starts to eat like he hasn't eaten in weeks. I take a small bite out of my burger. It's warm and juicy and yummy, but I'm not that hungry.

"So how are you doing?" he asks, wiping ketchup drips off his chin with the back of his hand. "Is physics blowing your mind?"

I shake my head and roll my eyes. "Physics is the easiest thing of all the things in my life right now."

He pops the last bite of his burger in his mouth and says, "Well, I guess that's good, then."

I shrug and put my burger on the crumpled bag. I stare across the street at the setting sun. The sky is turning bloodred and orange. It's beautiful. "How come I never knew your name was Billy?" I ask.

Twitch squints and turns his head a little to the side. "Are you asking me why you don't know my name? Because I don't know how to answer that." He laughs quietly.

"I just mean . . . did Clara call you Billy or Twitch? I never heard her call you Billy."

"Are you talking about her letter? The part about asking me to a dance?"

Now it's my turn for my cheeks to turn pink.

Billy looks at his sneakers. They're old black Converses, and he's drawn a super-cool-looking, intricate pattern all over the white rubber that covers his toes and the sides of the shoes. "When we were together, just the two of us hanging out, she called me Billy. But when we were with other people she called me Twitch like everyone else." His finger traces the designs on his shoe. He pinches his lips together in a straight line and looks up at me.

"Pretty sure I came by to see how *you* were doing. And now we're talking about me. How do you do that, Amelia? You're some kind of magician."

"You don't want to talk about this, huh?" I say. I understand.

"Are you going to eat that?" Twitch points at my burger with only one sad bite taken out of it. "You can have it," I say. "I had a sandwich over at Grant's not too long ago."

Twitch nods and takes my burger. He eats it slower as we both watch the sky changing colors. "So you're doing fine in physics, then?" he asks finally, swallowing the last bite.

"The physics part is fine," I say, watching a cloud race by. "It's just . . . I guess I never thought about the fact that the class would be full of kids who used to have class with Clara."

"Yeah," Twitch says. "Welcome to my life."

"Do you want to go to Kite Night with me?" I blurt.

"Huh?" He turns and looks at me.

"The stupid town party thing—"

"By the fountain, with all nighttime kite flying and the terrible DJ and the corn dogs? Yes, I know what Kite Night is, I just mean . . . uh . . . no offense, but . . ."

"Uuugh, nooooooo." I shove his shoulder hard. "Not like a date, dummy. Just, will you go with me?" I reach into my pocket and pull out Clara's letter. I unfold it and point to number three.

3) Ask Billy to a dance. (OMG. Billy. Sigh.)

He flushes, and his mouth opens and closes without making any sound.

"It's. Not. A. Date. Dummy," I say very slowly. "Boys. Are. Gross. And. Girls. Run. The. World. But. Please. Help. Me. Cross. One. Stupid. Thing. Off. This. List. Please."

"Okay, okay, you don't have to turn into a robot. Fine. But it's not a date. Sophomores don't date middle-school kids."

"It's not a date!" I shout. That makes Tiny bark from all the way in Mr. Robertson's backyard.

Twitch laughs. "Fine, fine. Excellent. Don't sic your dog on me."

"Not my dog." I laugh. "But I will if I have to."

Twitch holds his hand out for a shake. "Yes, Amelia Peabody, I will go with you to Kite Night so that you can cross one stupid thing off your list."

"Excellent," I say, and we shake hands so hard his helmet wobbles.

Twitch's phone chirps and he looks down at the

screen. His eyes widen for just a second and then go back to normal. "I gotta jet. But you're okay, yeah?"

I nod. "You're okay?"

He nods and stands up.

"Wait!" I say. "I'll be right back." I run into the house, upstairs to my room, and back down in record time. I hand him the softball and two gloves. "You left these the other day."

He takes them from me. "Aha! I was looking all over for them. Thanks."

And then he's off, skating down the street, gloves on both hands like a dork, ball nestled in one glove, empty Big Boy Burger bag stuffed in his back pocket.

CHAPTER FIFTEEN

"YOU DID NOT."

"I did."

"You did not."

"I did! Also, I'm having déjà vu."

Taylor shoves a book into her locker and primps in the mirror that hangs next to a picture of Beyoncé.

"Well, was it weird? Did you get nervous? I can't believe you guys are dating." She makes a face in the mirror like she smelled a spoiled hot dog. Though her eyes are sharp and pointy as her reflection stares at me standing behind her.

"I told you. It's not a date."

"Well, then it doesn't count." She slams her locker shut and smacks her lip gloss.

"Of course, it counts," I say. "The letter didn't say 'Ask Billy on a date,' it just said 'dance.'"

Taylor makes a gimme motion with her hand and

I sigh. I pull the letter out of my pocket and hand it to her. "Exhibit A," she says, jabbing at the letter with her finger. " 'OMG.' " She looks at me pointedly. "And exhibit B." She jabs with her finger again. " 'Sigh.' " She folds up the letter and hands it back to me. "She was clearly . . . feeling *feelings* for him, Amelia. It has to be a date." She stops walking dead in the center of the hallway and I run into her. She whips her head around to stare at me. "You ARE sure Twitch is the right Billy, aren't you?" She wrinkles up her nose. "It's just very hard to believe."

"Yes, he's Billy. No, it's not a date. Yes, it still counts." I'm starting to get irritated with Taylor. Has she always been this bossy?

"I'll see you at gym." I wave as I walk away, my back to her.

"Are we running tonight?" she calls after me.

"Sure!" I yell over my shoulder. Though I'm not really sure I want to.

When I get to class, I see everyone through the skinny window in the door. They're chatting and goofing around, waiting for the late bell to ring. Some kids sit on the desks and laugh at things on their phones. Others stand in a cluster at the back of the room. Everyone is either paired off, like Lacy and Katherine (*how* do they get so many classes together?!), or in a group, and I know that in about two minutes they'll all have to be in their seats when the bell rings, but still. Two minutes of standing in there, not in a group or paired off, is basically two lifetimes. I don't think I can open the door and go in. Geography isn't calling to me today. I turn quickly and walk down the hall. There are still a bunch of kids milling around, so no one notices as I walk past. I don't turn around, I don't look to the side. I just keep walking, holding my breath, until I walk out the hallway door into the bright afternoon sun.

When I get past the open expanse of the soccer field, I see a cluster of trees and I take a deep breath. I move past the tree line, and then, dropping my backpack against the trunk of a tree, I slide down next to it, sitting in a pile of leaves.

I've never skipped class before. I have no idea what will happen if I get caught. Mom and Dad are already mad because I wouldn't go to the lake last night. I'm not sure they'll even know how to punish me if they find out about this. I'm the good girl. Clara was the handful.

I pull my knees up to my chest, hugging them. Am I really going to sit out here and stare at trees for forty-five minutes? Great plan, Amelia. This is definitely more constructive than actually learning something about geography. I sigh. It's not like I can just march back into class, though, can I? Why didn't I hide in the bathroom and go in after the late bell? I would have missed the two lifetimes of not talking to anyone, but I wouldn't be sitting out here like a dope. Maybe I can go back in and tell Mr. Holbrook I was in the bathroom. Or maybe I'll just stay out here and listen to the tree whispers instead of listening to the class whisper about me.

I'm rummaging around in my backpack, trying to find a granola bar and a book when I hear a crunch. My heart stair-steps into my throat. Wonderful. Now I'm going to be killed by an ax murderer. My palms start to sweat as I hold my breath and try not to make any noise. The crunching sounds are getting louder. And now I hear voices. One voice in particular sounds familiar.

Through the brush, I see three or four figures pushing their way into the woods. They aren't super close, so I don't think they've seen me. I hear laughing and a sound like someone is shaking a spray-paint can. I catch a flash of red and white from the edges of a skating helmet, and yep. That's Twitch. I can't really see who's with him because they're walking fast. Soon they're deep in the woods and I can't hear them or see them anymore. Wonder what they're up to. A small part of me wants to follow them, but a bigger part of me is feeling a wash of exhaustion after the rush of terror. I should get back to class.

I sigh and zip up my backpack. At the edge of the trees, I look around to see if anyone's outside, but the coast is clear. I run up to the door I came out of and bounce off it when I push on the handle. Of course, it's locked. Uh-oh. I didn't think about that. I run to another door and it's locked, too. How in the world am I supposed to get back inside?!

Like some kind of inept spy, I run along the side of the school trying every door, but they're all locked. The only choice is to go in through the front door, and I know from coming to school late after various dentist appointments and things, *that* door is locked, too. The front office people have to buzz you in. I look at my watch. Twenty minutes until gym.

I go hide under the bleachers and watch everyone run track for the next ten minutes. Coach blows her whistle and the girls line up to go through the double doors that lead directly into the locker room. Luckily, Coach goes in ahead of everyone. I jump in at the back of the line and sneak in.

"Amelia? What in the world are you doing?" Georgia, who has been holding the door for everyone, seems to have a voice louder than anyone else in humankind.

I hold my finger to my lips. "I'm working in the office this period, and I have a message for Coach." I pull Clara's letter from my pocket and wave it. "Very important. Top secret."

"Uh," Georgia says, but I just walk briskly past her. I find an empty toilet stall and hide in there until the bell rings.

Once everyone is mostly out and the next class starts trickling in, I flush the toilet and emerge, somewhat victorious.

"Amelia?" Taylor's voice is behind me, and it sounds aghast. "What in the *world*?"

"What?" I whip around, startled.

"Girl." Taylor shakes her head. "I just . . . *what* is going on with you?"

That's when I catch a glimpse of myself in the mirror. My hair is full of leaves. Leaves and twigs are snagged all over the back of my sweater. I look like I've just crawled in from the woods. Which I have.

Taylor picks leaves out of my hair as I walk to my gym locker and pull out my sweats. She opens her mouth to say something, but I hold up a hand. "I don't want to talk about it."

"Okay," she says with a small laugh, though her expression is concerned. "I'll see you outside."

Amelia Peabody: the only person in the history of time who can calculate gravitational potential energy but who can't calculate how to correctly skip one class.

CHAPTER SIXTEEN

"IS IT EVEN SWIMMING SEASON?" I ask. "Is anyone even *going* to the lake these days?" I can hear the whine in my voice.

"That's where they're filming the contest, Amelia. What can I do?" Dad throws his arms out in a help-less gesture.

"You could not be part of the contest," I mutter under my breath. Then I say it louder, because why not? "Why do you even *have* to do the contest?" I ask. "It's just some silly TV show."

Dad pulls his face back like I slapped him. His voice is quiet. "Because it's my dream to have a successful barbecue business? Because I want to provide for you and Mom? Because it will make me happy?"

"Doesn't anyone in this house care about what would make ME happy?" I shout. It's like I'm floating above myself and watching the scene. I can't even believe these words are coming out of my mouth. It's so stereotypical. So teenager-y. And yet . . . it's how I feel. *Don't* they care about me? Don't they see how *un*happy it makes me to even *talk* about the lake, God forbid go there. I make a loud harrumph noise. "Even my *thoughts* are italicized. *That's* how upset I feel."

Mom stares at me. She seems to be wavering between anger and sadness. Dad is clearly settling in for full-on anger.

"I have to go practice for softball tryouts." I storm out of the kitchen and onto the front porch.

"Who ARE you?!" Dad shouts after me. "Be home by seven!"

Be home by seven? He's not going to march out here after me and drag me kicking and screaming to the lake? Of course not. I know Dad would never do that. But still. Did I just win that argument? I feel very uneasy as I run down to the alley behind the General Store where Taylor's "front door" is.

I knock on the door but no one answers. Weird. I know we had plans to run this evening. I jog in place for a minute and try to figure out what to do. I'm definitely not going home. And by myself, I don't know if I have the oomph to force myself to keep running when I want to give up. Hmm.

An idea lights up my brain. Perfect.

* * *

"Amelia? What are you doing here?" Twitch is standing in the doorway holding a bowl of ice cream. He looks different and I can't quite figure out why. Aha. It's his jaggedly crazy hair. He looks like a completely different person without that shark-bite helmet.

"Are you eating ice cream for dinner?" I ask, jogging in place.

"Are you jogging on my front porch?"

A voice from inside the house yells, "Who is it, William?"

"Amelia, Mom!" Twitch shouts back.

"Amelia Peabody?" Twitch's mom comes up behind him, wiping her hands on a dish towel. She sees me and smiles. It's that sad smile I know sooooooooo well. "How *are* you? How are your parents?"

"She's fine, everyone's fine," Twitch says. He hands her his bowl and shuts the door behind him before she can say anything else.

"Twitch!" I laugh. "I mean *William*! That was so rude! Also, how many names do you *have*?"

"Well, she was asking personal questions," he says, shaking his head. "And Billy is a nickname for William. Twitch is a nickname for, uh, everything." A tiny smile plays at the corners of his mouth.

"She was just asking how I am," I start, but he holds up his hand and I laugh. "Okay, yes, I saw the look in her eyes. The 'here's the girl with a dead sister' look. I am very familiar with it."

"Well, you're welcome for saving you from it," he says. I give him a little bow and say thanks.

"Do you want to play catch?" I ask. "I have been stood up for my jogging date with Taylor."

"Sure," Twitch says. "Don't move." He runs into the house and in a minute he's back out with the gloves and a ball. "You know you're going to have to get your own glove if you make the team."

"Details," I say, with a dismissive wave. We both laugh.

We go out into the street to throw the ball. I want to ask him what he was doing in the woods during school hours, but if I ask him then he'll know *I* was in the woods during school. Conundrum.

Mostly, we just play catch in silence. It's really, really nice. He seems to be kind of lost in his own thoughts, but I don't mind. No one is pestering me with questions, no one is giving me looks of pity or confusion. It's just catch. Plain and simple. My mind thinks: THROW and then it thinks CATCH and that's it. I wish I could do this forever.

"THERE YOU ARE, YOU DWEEB!"

My head swivels around. Taylor is jogging up the street. "Where have you been?" She's out of breath and sweaty.

"I went to your apartment and you weren't there," I say, confused.

"I was waiting at Deadman's Hill. Where we said we would meet." Her hands are on her hips. Twitch wanders over to us.

"What's up, Taylor?"

"My blood pressure, *Twitch*," Taylor says with an edge to her voice. "Amelia asked me to help her train for softball tryouts, but when we do train together, all she does is complain. And now today, she left me high and dry." She taps her foot angrily. "Looks like she found a more appealing trainer."

"What?" I say. "No! Taylor, come on." Why is she acting so mad?

"No, it's cool. Play catch with your boyfriend, Amelia. I get it." She runs off before I can say anything else.

I whip around just as Twitch is about to say something. "I've told her a million times you're not my boyfriend."

Twitch looks relieved, then says, "Do you need to go? Talk to her?"

I shake my head. "I do not. Now get back to where you were."

"Yes, ma'am," he says, and jogs back to his spot. I throw the ball way off to the side and he has to chase after it. Ugh. Stupid Taylor, ruining my Zen. But I do feel bad. Did I say I was going to meet her at the hill? I can't remember.

For the next few minutes, Twitch and I make a feeble attempt at throw and catch, catch and throw, but both of our minds are somewhere else now. Finally, I toss the ball back to Twitch, then I toss the glove.

"I gotta go," I say. "Thanks for practicing with me."

"No problem," Twitch says. "See you tomorrow."

"Bye." I watch him lope up the porch stairs and through the front door. It's dusk out now and the lights inside the house seem extra bright. I see Twitch go into the kitchen and say something to his dad. His two older sisters are sitting on the couch still in their soccer gear. His mom walks by the front window, sees me staring, and waves. Her wave startles me. She makes a gesture for me to come in, but I shake my head and run off like some kind of feral cat.

CHAPTER SEVENTEEN

SOMETIMES, DURING CLASS, I FIND myself mesmerized by Mr. Robertson's mustache. It is very, very shiny and very, very black. I wonder if it ever tickles him. I wonder if he has some kind of special mustache oil or shampoo to make it that shiny. I wonder if he goes out with friends and tries to pick up ladies and the ladies are all, "Oh, Mr. Robertson, you seemed like a regular man until you turned around and, *wham*, your mustache rays pierced my heart."

"Amelia?"

I blink. Everyone is staring at me. "Uh . . ."

Mr. Robertson taps at a formula on the whiteboard. "Can you . . ."

"The frequency of sound is . . ." I look over the numbers and do some calculations in my head, "292.66 hertz," I say quickly, solving the formula.

"I just wanted to know if you could name the

formula, Amelia." Mr. Robertson crosses his arms. "But good work solving it." He's eyeing me like he can't tell whether he should be mad at me for not paying attention, or impressed I could do the math in my head.

"Oh," I say. "Sorry. That's the Doppler shift formula." The class is all staring at me like my hair is on fire. I want to say, "What? *I'm good at physics.*" But I don't. Mr. Robertson's mustache quivers just a little bit as it does a bad job of hiding a smile.

I wonder where Twitch is today. It's weird sitting here at our table without him. I feel exposed or something, which is an irritating feeling. It's not like he's my protector, except that sometimes he is. I like it that he steers conversations away from uncomfortable things, and that he includes me in other things. I'm not some freakazoid middle-school physics genius to him, I'm just another kid in class. The way he treats me like a normal human seems to make other people treat me like a normal human, too. Without him here, I feel like my normal human mask is hanging off just enough to show the weirdo underneath.

As if my brain conjured him out of thin air, he bursts through the door, out of breath and sweating, drops his bag on the ground next to our table, and straddles his stool. He stares directly at my textbook, and my notebook, then grabs his own notebook and starts working on the problems on the page without saying a word.

"Ahem." Mr. Robertson looms over our table. I can smell Twitch's spicy boy smell mixed with something else . . . what is it? Nail polish? I look at his hands. His fingertips are red and blue. It's not nail polish, though. It's spray paint. Twitch stands up and follows Mr. Robertson to his desk, where they have a very quiet, but very heated, conversation. Twitch comes back to the table, grabs up his stuff, and storms out of the classroom.

Later, when the bell rings and I'm zipping up my backpack, Mr. Robertson strolls over, hands in his pockets. "How are you?" he asks. He jangles change in his pocket. That is maybe the only thing I don't like about Mr. Robertson. He's a change jangler.

"Fine," I say.

"Class treating you well?" *Jangle, jangle.* "You seem to be thriving." *Jangle, jangle.* His shiny mustache bends light toward his mouth, making his bottom lip shine, too.

"I love it," I say. "Really."

"Good," he says. "I'm glad to hear it." *Jangle, jangle.* I want to reach over and grab his hand out of his pocket to make him stop.

I throw my backpack over my shoulder and head to the door.

"Amelia," he calls after me. *Jangle, jangle.* "You make such good calculations in class, be sure to think carefully about the calculations you make outside of class, too. Think of the butterfly effect and how decisions you make now might affect your whole future." *Jangle.*

"Uh, okay," I say as I walk into the hallway. "Bye, Mr. Robertson. See you tomorrow." What in the world is he talking about? What calculations am I making outside of physics? Other than the fact that I'm calculating right now how to steal all of his change to keep it quiet.

The halls are full of kids flooding out of school, and I join the flood. My mind is wandering to what grilled cheese special is on the board at the General Store today, when I see Twitch duck out a side door with a couple of other kids. Hmm. I calculate that I want to follow him.

I wait a few seconds and then peek my head out the door. Twitch and the kids are walking toward the woods. I slip out of the door and try to quietly run close enough to them to see where they're going, but not be seen by them. Not an easy task when you're crossing a soccer field. They walk fast and I have to kind of run/skip to not lose them. I'm not even sure why I'm following them.

Out of nowhere I realize that, even though I am

constantly reminding Taylor that Twitch and I are just friends, I've always thought of him as *Clara's* friend. And while I want to know why Clara treated him the way she did, but still seemed to crush on him, I also just . . . well . . . I just want to know more about him. He's becoming more of *my* friend and less of Clara's former friend. And even though we aren't *best* friends or anything, it feels weird to realize he does things that I don't know about. That sounds very stalker-ish, but it's true. I just . . . I want to know what Twitch is up to.

We're in the woods now, and I'm trying to keep up without making a huge racket. It's pretty useless, though. Twigs break under my feet, and I trip at least nineteen times and go "OOF" each of those nineteen times. So it isn't a surprise when I hear a girl's voice, "Come on over, whoever you are. You are a terrible spy." Some people laugh.

I feel my face burn as I catch up to them. Twitch is standing in a small clearing with two girls, a guy, and someone whose back is to me. That person is bent over something and is shaking a spray-paint can.

"Amelia?" Twitch's face crinkles up in confusion as he sees me emerge from the trees. He's flanked by the girls, who both have their arms crossed. One has fiery dyed-red hair in a Mohawk. The other has a completely shaved head and huge silver hoop earrings.

"I . . ." I start. But I only now see everything surrounding us. There are tiny rocks creating a mosaic on the ground. It isn't finished, but it's huge and it takes my breath away. It's painted a deep, dark blue; the kind of blue that looks like it goes on forever and ever. Scattered everywhere in the blue are tiny golden stars. I can't tell if they're painted or if they're actual little stars glued onto the rocks. I squat down. They're painted. Whoa. So many of them. And around the edge of the whole thing is a red rim and white jagged triangles. I stand up so I can get a better view. Is it . . . teeth? It's like the shark teeth around Twitch's helmet. Am I standing in a giant deep-blue mouth filled with stars?

"I was actually going to bring you here," Twitch says after clearing his throat. "But I wanted it to be finished first."

That's when I realize the girl with the Mohawk is Maureen. And the bald girl is Desiree. They were on the boat with Twitch at Clara's party. The boy is Henry. The other boy stands up and wipes his hands on his pants. Jake. Everyone stares at me through the shadows of the trees. They were all on the boat when Clara drowned. I haven't seen them together since the funeral.

"We're getting really close to being finished," Twitch says. "Remember all those papers I dropped when we ran into each other at school ages ago? That was a bunch of research into figuring out how we can get city funding for an art project . . . maybe move this somewhere where other people can see it. Or maybe leave it here, but protect it. Anyway, we've been getting together more often lately so we can finish it." Twitch sighs and looks off into the distance. After a second he turns back to me. "We needed to do something. For Clara. Together. And we didn't know what. This just kind of . . . happened."

I can't quite figure out what I'm feeling. I want to cry. Not because I'm sad. I mean, I'm *always* sad, but I'm not extra sad or anything. I just . . . I think maybe I feel left out. No one thought to ask if I wanted to help? Just like Clara, this art that they've created for or about or because of her is so beautiful . . . and a little bit scary, and . . . familiar to me. But no one wanted to tell me about it until it was finished? They didn't even think to include me. Would Twitch have planned to tell me about it if we hadn't become quasi-friends?

I look at them all looking at me. Then I turn and run.

CHAPTER EIGHTEEN

I'VE SLOWED TO A WALK now that I've made it to the town square. I'm making my way to Grant's, brain still whirling, when I see Mrs. Grant pop out of the Enchanted Florist. She's holding two bunches of yellow flowers that look like daisies.

"Swamp sunflowers," Mrs. Grant says to me when we meet on the sidewalk. "Terrible name, beautiful flowers. Thought I'd spruce up the place a bit." She puts her hand on my arm. "Amelia, dear, are you all right? You look like you've seen a ghost."

I shake my head. I can feel hot tears swirling into my eyes. Stupid. It's stupid to cry. What am I even crying *about*?

"Here," Mrs. Grant says, handing me one of the bunches of flowers. She links her empty arm in mine. "Let's walk and talk."

"But the store . . ." I start. She shushes me.

"The store doesn't need a walk and talk right now. You do."

All I can do is nod and feel the tears spill down my cheeks, hot with anger over crying again, and also hot with, what . . . sadness? Left out–ness? Aloneness? Maybe that's it.

"I feel like there's no place for me," I whisper, my chin trembling. "I feel like everyone has a spot in the world. But I don't. It's like Clara and I shared a spot and when she died I lost my place, too. But that's not like Taylor, who has so many friends and always knows what she wants and how to get it. It's not like Twitch, who has these friends who are all creating art together. It's not like Dad and his barbecue, or you and your store, or Mom and her work. I don't have anything. I just float around and feel sad and invisible."

Mrs. Grant tightens her arm around mine. "Does it help if I tell you everyone is sad in their own way, and you are definitely not invisible?"

I shrug. As we're walking, a bunch of workers are setting everything up for Kite Night. It's really coming up so soon?

Our walk and talk mostly ends up just a walk as we make a loop around the town center in companionable silence. When we get to Grant's General Store, I feel better, even though there wasn't a lot of soul-searching or talking. Sometimes just walking with someone is nice. Kind of like just playing catch.

"Amelia!" Taylor screeches as soon as we walk through the door. My peacefulness shatters. "Now you're out exercising with *Gram* instead of me?! Do you even *want* my help anymore?!" She glowers at me for a split second and then storms upstairs before I even have a chance to respond.

"I don't think she's used to seeing you on your own so much," Mrs. Grant says, pulling on an apron over her sweater and jeans. "Give her time. She'll figure it out."

I'm not sure I want to give her time to figure it out, though. It's annoying to always be yelled at, especially when I don't feel like I've done anything to deserve the yelling. I've seen her at school with Lacy and Katherine. It's not like she's pining away for me, or something. She has plenty of friends and projects and things. Can't we be friends without her having to know about every tiny thing I do?

Taylor comes back downstairs holding Ratface. She bites her lip and takes a deep breath. "Sorry I just yelled at you. That wasn't very cool. I just . . . I'm here to help you, Amelia, you know that, right?"

"Of course, I know that," I say, feeling like maybe I have whiplash from her mad–not mad switcheroo.

"And you know that sometimes I have to figure things out on my own, right?"

She nods, but she doesn't look convinced. Ratface leaps out of her arms and runs to the front door to greet a customer.

"Why don't you two get behind the counter, wash your hands, and help me cut some cheese?" Mrs. Grant asks.

Taylor and I both burst out laughing, and for just a second it feels like old times.

CHAPTER NINETEEN

"COME ON," I SAY. "TAYLOR. This is stupid." We're standing in her kitchen. She's draped red fabric over the window so that the small area glows like the inside of an eyelid. There's a long tablecloth hanging off the kitchen table and a candle in the middle. On one end of the table is a Ouija board.

"No, Amelia. You need closure. We're going to fix you for good." She smiles brightly and gestures to a chair nearest the board.

I sit and cross my arms. "Um, (*a*), I don't need to be fixed. And (*b*), this is a game, Taylor. There's no such thing as ghosts."

Taylor sits across from me and shakes her head like I just told her the earth is flat. "Girl, all you ever DO is talk about how you wish you could stop feeling sad, how you wish you could be normal, how you wish you could be as beautiful as me." I stick my tongue out at her, but I smile a little bit. She's such a booger, but I do love her. "This is your brief opportunity to break through the bonds of this world," she continues with a twinkle in her eye, "and peek through the veil of the next world. This is your chance to have some new last words with Clara." Her voice has softened and she puts a hand over mine. "Okay? I know it's silly, but maybe it will help?"

I nod, and swallow back tears. It's stupid. But fine. Taylor deserves a normal friend, and I would love to launch into the world of Taylorville where everything is fun and no one is sad and the only thing that makes me angry is when my best friend doesn't exercise enough.

"So, what do we do?" I ask.

The Ouija board has the alphabet in the middle of it, split into two lines and bent in a kind of rainbow shape. Under the alphabet is a line of numbers going from one to nine, with a zero at the end, and under that it says GOOD BYE. It says YES and NO in the top corners. There's a plastic thing in the middle of the board that's sort of in a heart shape, and in the middle of it is a magnifying glass so you can see what's under it.

"Put two of your fingers here," Taylor says, showing me how to hold the plastic thing. "And I put two of my fingers *here*," she says, putting her hand on the other side of it. We look up at each other and burst out laughing.

"Dumb . . ." I say with a smile.

"Zip it, you," Taylor says. But she's smiling, too. "Make sure you don't push it or anything. Just let your fingers barely rest there."

We sit like that for a second. "Now what?" I say. The red light filtering in probably isn't any warmer than usual, but I'm starting to feel hot and claustrophobic in the small kitchen. I'm ready to get this thing done. I need closure for my closure.

Taylor makes a face. "The instructions weren't in the box. So . . . I guess we just ask questions?" She clears her voice, and in a very dramatic voice says, "Hello, spirit world. I hope you are doing well today. We would like to talk to Clara Peabody. Is she available?"

"It's not a voice mail—" I start to say, but the plastic thing under our fingers jerks over to the YES by a drawing of a smiley sun. What the—?

Taylor and I lock eyes. "Oh em gee," she whispers. "Spirit world," she continues in her silly deep voice. "Just to confirm we have the right Clara, can she tell us her sister's name?" The plastic thing glides under our fingers to the A. Then it jerks to the M and my heart starts to bang in my chest like I've just sprinted half a mile. When it moves toward the E, I yank my hand off of it, my eyes meeting Taylor's in a kind of panic.

"This isn't real," I say. "This can't be . . ."

"Put your hand back on it, Amelia," Taylor says. Her voice is firm, but not mean. "This is your chance to talk to Clara. Make things right."

I swallow hard. How can this be real? There's no such thing as the spirit world or ghosts or any of that. When you die, you die. I have seen death. There is no filmy fog of a soul floating up to the sky. And yet . . .

My voice comes out as a croak. "Clara? Do you hate me?"

The plastic thing pulls our fingers to the NO, and I feel something inside me break open. A rush of tears pours down my face. I stare at the board and sob, "I had no idea you were going to die. I was mad you wouldn't let me on the boat. I didn't actually mean I never wanted to see you again. I didn't actually mean I hated you."

The plastic thing moves to *I*, then *K*, then *N*, then *O*, and finally *W*. It stops for a second, and Taylor and I just look at each other, stunned. I feel movement under my fingers and now it moves to *L*, and *O*, and *V*, then *E*. Then it slowly moves to *U*.

I bury my face in my hands and cry and cry. Can this be real? Is it actually Clara speaking to us from . . . wherever? Does she really not hate me? I'm sniffling and wiping my face as Taylor stands up and comes over to me. She kneels next to me and puts her arm around my shoulders. She's about to say something, when a streak of white light crashes into the kitchen. Our red eyelid opens to reveal Mrs. Grant standing in the doorway at the top of the stairs from the store.

"What in the world?" she says. Ratface runs past her and over to us, wagging his tail and hopping around.

"Ratface, no!" Taylor hisses, making a grab for him. She misses, though, and he runs under the hanging tablecloth, barking. The tablecloth ripples as he runs around under the table. Now he's growling and barking and I hear . . . what was that? A "*shhh*"? From *under* the table? Wait. What?

I hear it again: "Shhh!" and that's when Taylor puts her hands over her face. Ratface is going absolutely berserk now and the shushes become "*ow!*" and "*stop it!*" Then the tablecloth lifts up and Twitch rolls out from under the table, Ratface attached to his back pocket, trying to free a stick of beef jerky. Twitch's helmet is all cockeyed on his head, and he's holding a big U-shaped magnet that I recognize from physics class.

Taylor peeks at me through her hands. My mouth hangs open. Twitch sits on the floor and says nothing. Mrs. Grant has her hands on her hips. Ratface eats the jerky.

Finally, I find my voice. "This was a JOKE? You were . . . You thought . . ." My face feels like it's going to catch on fire.

"Amelia," Taylor pleads. "It wasn't a joke, I swear. We just wanted to—"

But I don't hear what she has to say. I don't WANT to hear it. I fling myself from my seat, and fly down the stairs. Taylor and Twitch call after me, but I don't turn around. I'm never speaking to either one of them again.

Ever.

CHAPTER TWENTY

HOW COULD THEY? HOW COULD they? I'm pacing circles in my bedroom, raging mad. I feel like every bond of friendship or trust or *anything* has been shattered into a billion tiny pieces.

When I came home, I flew past Mom, who was at the kitchen table reading and having a snack. She called upstairs after me, but I didn't answer. Now she's knocking quietly on my door.

"Amelia? Taylor's here."

"NO!" I yell, spluttering. I'm so mad I can't even find complete sentences. I have turned into a cavewoman. A very, very angry cavewoman. "GO!" I shout, pointing at the dresser shoved in front of the closed door. "GET OUT! AAAARGH!"

"Amelia?" Taylor's voice is small outside my door. I want to destroy something. I breathe fire and smoke as I cast my gaze around the room. It lands on a picture of me and Taylor making goofy faces. I tear it up into tiny shreds and then shove the tiny shreds under the corner of the bottom of the door that isn't covered by the dresser.

"I was just trying to help," Taylor says through the door. "I thought this would fix everything. I thought it would make you . . . you . . . again."

The rage inside me, which I thought had already hit "exceeds maximum," boils up even faster and angrier. "THIS IS ME!" I scream. "I AM ME! I CAN'T BE FIXED! THIS IS WHAT YOU GET! THIS BIG MESS OF A PERSON IS ME NOW! THE ME I WAS ISN'T THE ME I AM ANYMORE!" The words I'm screaming make perfect sense to me, but I can hear how they might sound like Dr. Seuss having a very bad day. I don't care. Taylor can figure it out.

"Amelia, please," Taylor says. "I wasn't trying to hurt you. I was trying to help." I can hear that she's crying, but I don't care. Good. Let *her* cry for once.

"Amelia." It's Mom now. "Take a deep breath, baby. Deep breaths."

There's some quiet talking that I can't understand, and I hear footsteps going down the stairs. After a minute, it's Mom again. "Taylor went home. Can you open the door now, please? Can you tell me what happened?"

I don't really want to tell Mom what happened,

but it crashes over me that I have zero friends now. And I really, really need to talk about what happened, if only to get the whole yucky story out of me. Like barfing when you've eaten bad fish. I push the dresser out of the way and open the door. Mom rushes in and grabs me in a bear hug. Neither of us says anything while I cry and cry until I can't anymore. Then we sit on my bed and I tell her the whole story.

Mom is quiet for a bit when I'm all talked out. Then she says, "Well, that was a very poor choice on their part."

I start to laugh through all my tears and snot. I wipe my face with the back of my hand and my voice comes out blurry, "You think?!"

Mom laughs, too, as she nods. "A terrible plan."

I lie back on my bed, my nose completely stuffed up from all the crying. "Why would they be so mean? Why would they do something like that?" My voice has gone from sounding blurry and wet to sounding like I have a very bad cold.

Mom lies back next to me and we both stare at the ceiling. "I think people are good at heart," she says quietly. "I think Taylor and William really were trying to help you, even though their execution was terrible. I think people who have not experienced hard things have a difficult time understanding what it's like, and so they might do or say things that feel insensitive. They might do or say things that ARE insensitive."

"But then is it my job to tell them that?" I ask. "I don't want that job. I want them to be able to figure it out on their own."

"I know, honey," Mom says, taking hold of my hand. "It shouldn't be your job or my job to comfort the people who are supposed to be comforting us. Grief is hard for everyone. It takes a toll."

I don't say anything. All the anger is slowly dissipating, like the steam on a road after a particularly violent thunderstorm.

"How could they do that, though?" I whisper.

"They just wanted to help," Mom whispers back.

"That's not good enough of an answer," I whisper.

"I know," Mom whispers back. And we lie there together, on my bed, until the sun sinks and the moon rises and Dad comes home, walks up the stairs, and stands in my doorway. Wood smoke drifts off of him.

"Everything okay in here?" he asks.

"Not really," I say.

He comes over and lies on top of us both, squishing us until we can't help but laugh and squeal for him to get off.

"I brought dinner," he growls into our hair, making us squeal and squirm more. His huge arms dig under us both until he's lying on us *and* hugging us, and all three of us are giggling. "Guess I better bring this giant, heavy cord of wood down to the smoker," he says, trying to lift us from the bed. "Guess it's time to see how this new flavor will rock everyone's taste buds." We're too heavy for him, or he pretends we are, or he loses his balance, I'm not sure which, but Dad makes a startled grunt and rolls off us onto the floor.

"Man down," he groans. "Man down."

Mom stands up and offers him a hand. I stand up and offer him my hand, too, and together we heave him to his feet.

He and Mom share a quick look that seems to say, "What in the world?" and "I'll tell you later, but it's okay now."

"Time to eat?" he asks.

"Let's eat," Mom says. She puts her hands on my shoulders, I put my hands on Dad's shoulders (which I can barely reach), and we conga-line down the stairs to the kitchen.

CHAPTER
TWENTY-ONE

"OKAY," MR. ROBERTSON SAYS, CLAPPING his hands loudly, one time. "Ready to shake things up a bit? How about we have a little fun for once?"

Someone interrupts, "But we always have fun in *your* class, Mr. Robertson!" and everyone laughs.

Mr. Robertson clears his throat and says in a deep, grave, booming voice. "Of course, you do." A few people whistle and hoot in excitement, but I have no idea why. Mr. Robertson continues in his grave voice, "For the next couple of classes, we are going to explore the physics behind ghost hunting." Someone who's sitting next to the light switch flashes the lights a couple of times and everyone laughs. I feel my heart start beating a little faster. "We're going to learn what exactly ghost hunters look for when they're searching for life after death, and we're going to use our scientific minds to ask ourselves: Can physics *really* explain the unexplainable?"

The class is full of murmurs and excitement. My mouth has gone dry. I can't believe this. It's like a *school-sanctioned* Ouija board unit. Now, more than ever, I don't want to think about ghosts. And even though I don't believe Clara is lurking somewhere in the clouds, I hate to even imagine the possibility she might be trapped somewhere trying to communicate with me but is unable to get through. Stupid Twitch and stupid Taylor made me think, for just a second, that she was out there somewhere, and it was both the most wonderful and most terrifying feeling ever. It makes my stomach flop just to remember.

"If the next few classes are going to make any of you uncomfortable," Mr. Robertson says, staring directly at me, "feel free to let me know after class. I can give you an alternative assignment and you can work independently in the library."

Yeah, great, like the girl who's already known as the One with the Dead Sister is really going to be the *only* one who excuses herself from ghost class. Can you *imagine* the pitying looks I'd get from everyone? Thanks to Twitch and Taylor, I know with absolute surety that ghosts don't exist. I can handle this.

* * *

The next day speeds by like a freight train headed for a cliff. It's the first time I've ever dreaded physics, and my feet drag as I walk over to the high school. The woods whisper in the wind off to the side, and I think about ducking in there to hide. But no. I trust Mr. Robertson. I think. I mean, physics is math. And math is solvable. No mysteries. Right? I take a deep breath. Everyone else might try to use these lessons to prove that ghosts exist, but I'm going to work to prove they don't. I square my shoulders and march into school.

Twitch is already at our table for once, and he looks at me like Ratface does after I yell at him for eating my shoelaces. Fine. Let him look that way. I'm never talking to him again, so he's just going to have to get used to it. I sit on my stool and turn my back to him so I don't have to see his dumb face or his stupid helmet or any of him at all.

Mr. Robertson launches into a lecture on Einstein's theory of relativity. He writes $E=MC^2$ on the board. He talks about how energy can neither be created nor destroyed, so does that mean once a person has been alive their energy is floating in a little ball somewhere, a ghost of their former selves?

I raise my hand. "Mr. Robertson, that's the dumbest thing I've ever heard." Everyone turns quickly to stare at me.

"Excuse me?" he says. His mustache is very, very sparkly today.

"Well, what I mean is . . ." I say, "if energy is neither created nor destroyed, then when we're created as humans we're using energy that's already been around, right? So when we die, that energy goes back to where it came from, don't you think? We all came from stardust, and we're all going back to stardust."

The class is completely silent.

"Stardust, huh?" Mr. Robertson says as my words hover over everyone.

Stardust.

Did I really just say that?

My mind immediately goes to the woods, to the tiny golden stars painted all over the mural. Is Clara stardust? I feel my eyes start to swim.

I gather up my stuff in a rush and dash out of the classroom.

"Amelia?" Mr. Robertson shouts after me, but I don't stop. I run all the way to the woods, pushing through the branches and leaves until I get to the right spot. I throw down my backpack and heave myself onto the rock next to the art project Twitch and everyone have been working on for so long.

I stare at the tiny stars, the deep blue, the jagged teeth.

Can Clara be nowhere and everywhere all at once?

Bits of dust float in the air, riding on sunbeams that cascade through the tree branches. They are golden, too, like tiny daytime stars taking flight. I hold my hand out, and the little bits of dust and dirt dance around my fingers in the brightness and heat of a slant of sun.

"Amelia."

It's Twitch, and he just about gives me a legitimate heart attack.

"TWITCH!" I shout, jumping up. "You scared me!" A wave of dizziness makes me wobble as my breath tries to catch up with my heart rate.

"Sorry," he says. "I'm sorry for everything."

I hold up my hand. I don't want to hear it.

"I—" he starts, but I point at him.

"No," I interrupt. "I don't want you here. I'm . . . I'm thinking about the theory of relativity, okay?"

He holds up his hands. "Fine. I'll leave you to think. But, Amelia, I really am very sorry." He pushes his way through the trees and is gone. I hate that my first instinct is actually to call him back over. I know I said I didn't want him here, but if I'm being honest with myself, I don't really want to be alone either. I don't call for him, though. I let him go.

"Oh, Clara," I whisper. "If you're everywhere, why do I feel so alone all the time?"

CHAPTER
TWENTY-TWO

"READY?" MOM PEEKS HER HEAD into my room.

I look up from the homework spread out all over my desk. "Not going," I say. "Why are *you* going? I thought you hated Kite Night."

Mom is awkwardly holding a box kite with reflective tape all over it. Her eyes are bright. "Dad was right about the lake. Maybe he's right about this, too. Why don't you come with us?"

"I was going to go," I say. "But ever since the thing with Taylor and Twitch, eh, I'm just not feeling it." Kite Night has never been a huge thing for me. Not like with Mom and Dad. I've seen pictures from when they were kids and went, and then the pictures from when they took Clara and me when we were super tiny. I guess it used to be a big deal for them. Mom hasn't been since . . . well . . . she hasn't been in a long time.

"Fair enough," Mom says, and I think I might fall out of my chair. She isn't going to argue with me? Tell me I need fresh air for a fresh soul or something silly like that? "If you change your mind, you know where to find us."

"Eating delicious corn dogs and flying ridiculous kites and winning at dancing!" Dad yells upstairs.

"If I change my mind, I know where to find you," I say. "Have fun. Don't get into any trouble."

Mom laughs. "We'll try not to. Though Dad is going to be handing out free samples of his bacon chocolate chip cookies, and I'm pretty sure he needs a permit for that."

"Then I'll be here to bail you out of jail if I have to," I say. Mom gives me a thumbs-up and pulls my door shut. Wow. That conversation was just . . . almost fun, and not full of arguing? Huh.

I look back down at my homework, but my concentration is broken. I take Clara's letter, which is getting pretty beat-up, and I flatten it out on my desk. It doesn't actually say "go to a dance with Billy," it just says ask him to a dance. So, technically, I can still cross this off the list, right? I'm mulling over the semantics when I hear a tap-tap-tapping at my window. I slide the curtains to the side just as a handful of pebbles scatter over the surface, sending me back on my heels, startled. I go closer to the window and look down.

Twitch.

He's pretending like he's going to throw the softball next. Down at his feet are two gloves. I shake my head. He makes an exaggerated pout. I shake my head harder. He falls to his knees and holds his hands up like he's begging or praying or both. I sigh and unlock the window. I push it open and stand there, hands on my hips, shivering in the breeze.

"Catch?" he shouts up at me.

I don't say anything.

"Come on, Amelia. Please? Just for a minute? It's about to get dark anyway."

In that moment I feel really, really tired. I don't want to hate Twitch. I don't want to hate Taylor. But what *do* I want? "Don't move," I say down to Twitch. I close the window, grab a sweater, and go downstairs. Once I'm on the front porch I wave at him to come over and sit beside me.

"Here's the thing," I say, after a few seconds of us sitting quietly next to each other. "I know you said you were sorry. I just . . . I don't know why it doesn't feel like enough. I don't know what to do about that."

Twitch tosses the softball from one hand to the other. "I could stand on Mr. Robertson's desk and shout to our whole physics class about how I did a stupid thing and now I'm sorry. I could take out an ad in the newspaper. I could invent a time machine, go back in time, not do the Ouija board thing, come back and tell you I didn't do it, and you'd be super confused because it had never happened. Though I guess if I invented a time machine, I'd go back and stop Clara from getting in that boat. But then you and I wouldn't be friends."

I snatch the ball from his hands. "Time travel is complicated."

"Everything is complicated," he says, standing up and putting on a glove. He jogs down the front walk and punches the glove. "Right here. Hit me as hard as you can."

I throw the ball with a ferocity I've never tried before, and it slams into the mitt with a satisfying *pow*. Twitch looks at me and smiles. "Again," he says.

Over and over I throw the ball as hard as I can, until I get lost in the rhythm. Wind up, release, step back, catch. My shoulder starts to ache, my fingers are going numb, but it feels incredible to fling this angry energy out of my body.

"Did I ever tell you why people call me Twitch?" Twitch asks, throwing the ball to me a little harder than before.

"No," I say.

"Clara never said anything about it?" *Wham*. The ball lands hard in my mitt.

"She didn't," I say, throwing it back.

"When we were in third grade, Clara and I were at school walking together to bring the attendance sheet to the front office when I collapsed. I don't remember it at all. I only remember waking up in the hospital after. It was my first epileptic seizure."

"You have *epilepsy*?" I had no idea. And now I feel this awful dripping, sinking feeling down to my toes because I know Clara, and I think I know where his story is going. The ball lands even harder in my glove, and my palm stings through the leather.

Twitch pushes up his sleeve and shows me the bracelet I've always seen but never paid close attention to. "That's why I wear this." Then he knocks on his ubiquitous shark-mouth helmet. "And this. Though, technically, my medicine works great now and I don't have to wear the helmet like when I was little. I still like it anyway. It makes me feel, I don't know, safe or something."

I toss the ball back. His Adam's apple bobs for a second, then he continues.

"Apparently, after the ambulance took me away, Clara told everyone I'd had a 'Twitchy attack.' She showed them how I'd seized up and shaken and wet my pants. When I came back to school a few days later, everyone welcomed me with imitations of my shaking and whispers about my pants wetting." The ball pounds into my glove. I throw it back and give my hand a shake, to try to disperse the painful tingles. "It took a while to get my epilepsy under control, so I had a few more seizures at school and I had to start wearing a helmet. A real freak show. And lots of Twitchy attacks to entertain my classmates."

"That's so awful," I say. "Why were you friends with her after that? Why do you let people call you Twitch?"

Twitch laughs, but it's sharp and not the ha-ha kind of laugh I usually hear from him. "There's not a lot of 'let' to it, Amelia. People are going to say what they're going to say. It took me a long time, but I learned that instead of getting mad, I had to take over the nickname on my own terms. Does that make sense?" The ball slams into my mitt and I wince.

"So, you asked them to stop and they didn't," I say.

"Yes, but it became more than that. I wanted to control this mean thing and turn it into something boring, something that would melt all the meanness out of it. So, they called me Twitchy, and I started calling myself Twitch. I turned it into something that belonged to me. I introduced myself that way to teachers and new kids and everyone. YOU didn't even know my name was Billy."

"That's because I didn't know Billy was a nickname for William!"

He smiles and shakes his head. "I took control of the name and, by doing that, I took away its power to hurt me. I was mad at Clara for a long time, but we were eventually friends again—because eventually I believed her when she said she was sorry, and because I took the thing she did to me and turned it into my own thing."

I toss the ball back to him even though it's getting super dark now and hard to see. I thought I'd known how his story was going to end, but I'd actually only figured out part of it. "Are you telling me that I should start calling myself Ouija and keep being mad at you for a while?" I try for a smile.

"No," he says, with a real laugh this time. "I'm saying that people can be mad at each other and they can forgive each other and they can be mad at each other again and they can do stupid things and they can do smart things. The best part of being a human, Amelia, is *being a human*. We are all whiteboards that can be covered in terrible words, erased, and re-covered in better words." I lower my glove a tiny bit, feeling that sink in, just as he throws the ball really fast. It clips the edge of my mitt, takes out the wind chimes hanging from the top of the porch, and smashes through the plate glass window right into the kitchen.

My mouth flies open as my head swings from Twitch to the smashed window and back to Twitch again. He drops his glove, runs up to me, and puts his hands on his head.

"I hope my parents are as good at forgiving as you are," I say as I start to laugh. Then he starts to laugh, too, and soon we're both buckled over laughing so hard we can barely breathe.

"Are you going to say, 'You should see the other guy'? Because I don't want to see the other guy," Dad says, coming up behind us. He's holding a couple of bags, and his arms hang limply at his sides. He gives Mom a helpless look. Her mouth hangs open much like mine and Twitch's just did.

"Are you at least friends again?" Mom says, rubbing her forehead.

Twitch looks to me and shrugs. I take a deep breath and say in a quiet voice, "Yes?"

"Well, good," Mom says. "Then it will be more fun when you rapidly, rapidly, RAPIDLY work together to raise the money to fix this."

"William," Dad says, shaking his head. "Go around back and find the big blue tarp in the shed. Amelia, go get the broom and dustpan." Dad goes inside, and Mom follows him. They drop the bags they're carrying and stare at us through the former window. "Go!" Dad says. It looks like he's trying to be mad, but really he wants to laugh. Kind of.

Twitch and I both disappear to the shed as fast as we can.

CHAPTER TWENTY-THREE

"GOOD MORNING, NOLAN RYAN," DAD says as he wanders downstairs and into the kitchen, still in his pajama pants. His hair stands up all over his head, making him look like a cartoon character that's just been struck by lightning.

"Who's Nolan Ryan?" I ask, pouring myself a glass of orange juice. The tarp covering the window makes an ominous *whap whap whap* noise as the wind outside tries to rip it loose from all the duct tape holding it to the window frame.

"Amazing pitcher for the Texas Rangers," Dad says. "Probably broke dozens of windows in his day." Dad is trying to start the coffee, but is not quite awake yet. Coffee beans go everywhere as he tries to pour them into the grinder, and he curses under his breath. Dad has never been much of a morning guy. For a while after Clara died, he wasn't an anything guy. He just never got out of bed. He got some medicine, though, to help with that, and now he's back to not being much of a morning guy.

"Technically, Twitch is Nolan Ryan, then," I say, helping him clean up the spilled coffee beans.

"Technically, I am going to flip my lid if we don't get this window fixed as soon as possible. Did you sleep at all last night?" He rubs his eyes, and I wonder if that same move is something he did when he was little. He kind of looks like a pouty kid right now.

I shrug. "I slept okay. Why?" Right on cue the tarp makes the *whap whap whap* noise again, and Dad gestures to it with a frustrated arm fling.

"That! That noise! All night, *whap whap whap*. I can't take it, Amelia."

"It's going to take a little while to figure out how to pay for a new window, though, Dad," I say, popping some bread into the toaster. "It's not like Twitch and I can just whip out a credit card and get it fixed."

Dad points at me and frowns. "I feel like your voice has more of an edge than it needs to, ma'am. You guys broke it, and you're going to have to pay for it. However"—his pointing hand is now stroking his beard thoughtfully—"I *do* have a credit card, so here's what's going to happen."

Mom comes downstairs now, all dressed for work. She steps on some coffee beans we missed and they crunch under her heels. She kisses me on the top of my head as she goes over to the coffeepot that is busy grunting and whirring as it works to create its addicting elixir.

Dad kisses Mom quickly and then turns his attention back to me. "I am going to pay for a new window. Think of it as a loan. You and Twitch will owe me the full amount of the bill. Possibly I will charge you interest."

I'm about to protest, but Dad holds up his hand. "In order to pay me back—and, Amelia, this is nonnegotiable—you and Twitch will work at Pits 'n' Pieces after school and on the weekends until your debt is paid."

"Ooh, good plan," Mom says, stealing a bite of my toast.

"What?!" I say, feeling my heart start to pound. "No! Not a good plan. Terrible plan. The worst plan. I can think of something better, just—"

Dad sits at the table across from me and puts both his hands on it, palms down. He stares at me. "Nonnegotiable," he says slowly and leans forward so that his nose is close to mine. "I am the boss of you still, and this is what I am currently bossing you to do." He sits back and crosses his arms over his chest, a look of satisfaction spreading across his face. Mom stares at him like she has no idea who he is, but she likes what she sees.

"After school. Today," Dad says, stabbing the table with his finger. "I'll call Twitch's parents to let them know."

"And I'll call Mrs. Grant to let her know you won't be at the store," Mom says.

I stand up in a huff, my chair squealing across the floor. "Not fair," I say, trying not to panic at the prospect of having to go to the lake TODAY. "Not fair!"

Dad lifts his hands in a "what are you going to do?" shrug. "We are all familiar with the unfairness of life, Amelia," he says. "I'll see you this afternoon."

I angrily gather up my school stuff and stomp out of the house. I turn back to see if Mom and Dad are gloating in the kitchen, but I only see the huge blue tarp mocking me. Aaaargh.

My pace is fast as I grouchily walk to school. I see Taylor walking ahead of me and think about running to catch up with her. Maybe she could help me figure out how to get out of going to the lake. But then I remember I'm mad at her. We have not yet broken a window together to make up. I sigh. I could run and catch up to her and tell her that I'm not mad anymore. I could ask her if we can go back to how everything was before. She glances back and sees me. I lift up my hand to wave, but she whips her head around and quickly jaywalks across the street to where Lacy and Katherine are motioning to her. Okay. Well, I guess we'll have to talk later. For just a second I allow myself to imagine chasing after her and blocking her path to Lacy and Katherine and making her talk to me, but then . . . ugh. Who can blame Taylor, really? For three years I've been a sad mess of a friend. No wonder they seem so shiny and fun. A rock would seem shiny and fun compared to me.

I slow down a little now, because I don't want to get to school too early. If I get there now, I'll just have to wander around and stare at everyone hanging out together and be reminded of my tragic lack of friends. So much for being the queen of eighth grade. I feel more like the court jester, except court jesters are funny. Maybe I'm the guy who sings all the sad songs at the big castle dinners. The one with the cautionary tales of woe.

The woods are to my left, with school looming up ahead. Maybe I could go back in the trees for a few minutes and take a closer look at the art Twitch has been working on with the other boat kids. Right at that moment the wind blows through the tops of the trees and it sounds like a quiet "Yesssssssss" being carried on the wind. My mind jumps to the Ouija board and I feel my pulse quicken. Then I remind myself all of that was fake and stupid. Clara is not trying to talk to me. It was just the wind. Even so, I feel compelled to tromp through the leaves and undergrowth. I mean, I could hide out in the middle of a forest, or be early to homeroom. The choice is not difficult, by my calculations.

It's a cloudy morning, and the cover of the trees makes it even darker. When I get to the clearing it looks different than last time. The blue is almost black and the stars don't glimmer. The red surrounding the edges is deep and bleeds into the white of the teeth. It feels sinister today instead of sparkly and amazing. It makes me think of the lake, actually, and how on a hot summer day it shines and shimmers like a giant has thrown a handful of glitter over the surface. But then, on cloudy days, or at night, the water looks fathomless and black, with an eerie stillness. It's so interesting how the same place can look so different.

I sit on a tree stump and run the sole of my shoe over the deep blue mosaic. They must have poured and smoothed concrete and then laid out all of these pebbles. Except, it looks like they painted the pebbles first, because when I lean closer I can see that the grout holding everything together is an ever darker blue. It is a magnificent piece of art, both beautiful and a little bit scary. Clara would have loved this. It's just like her.

"They're making me go to the lake today," I whisper. The trees rustle around me. I pull Clara's letter from my pocket. "I've been trying to do some things for you," I say, still whispering. "I figured out who Billy is, and by the way, you were super mean to him when you guys were small. I can't believe he forgave you." The painted stars sprinkled throughout the blue are different sizes. I didn't really notice that before. I stand up and walk around the edge of the giant mouth. "I've been training for softball tryouts, too. How crazy is that?" I look up at the trees blowing in the wind. "Probably not as crazy as talking to myself in the woods."

I fold up the letter and put it back in my pocket. "I don't know about throwing a party, though. I don't actually have any friends, expect for Twitch. And I don't know if I can be nicer to Mom, because she's colluding with Dad to make me go to the lake." I'm quiet for a minute, just listening to the trees. "I miss you," I say, my voice the smallest of whispers. Then, out of nowhere, there's a huge crack of thunder so loud I can feel it slam into my chest. I duck instinctively, grabbing on to the stump I was sitting on a minute ago. As soon as the reverberations from the thunder stop, buckets of rain start to fall. It's a deluge, what my grandmother would have called a frog strangler. And even sheltered by the trees, I'm getting sopping wet. I grab my backpack and run from the woods, knowing that when lightning strikes, you do not want to be standing under tall things that can transfer that electricity to your body. Of course, you also don't want to be the tallest thing running back to school.

I burst from the edge of the trees just as it starts to rain even harder. I'm soaked to the bone now and laughing hysterically. Twitch and I won't be working at Pits 'n' Pieces today, because Dad doesn't open the trailer in weather like this. No lake for me! Unless you count the lakes growing in my shoes.

I'm laughing and running and I'm sure I look like a crazy person, but I don't care. I stumble up the stairs to the front entrance of school, but the doors are locked. What! I look at my watch. Oh my gosh, I'm fifteen minutes late. Is there some kind of time warp in the woods?! I pound the buzzer and wave to a woman in the front office who sees me standing there, drenched. She buzzes me in and I bolt through the door, running to class. I slip and slide the whole way, my shoes having turned into skates.

I barrel into homeroom and squelch into my seat, also trying to squelch my hiccupping laughter. Taylor stares at me with her mouth open, as does pretty much everyone except for Mrs. Henderson, who apparently didn't see or hear me come in. How is that possible?

She's writing something on the board about parent-teacher conferences.

I lean back in my seat, water pooling on the floor around me, and I smile at the ceiling. I totally don't believe in ghosts or the afterlife or anything like that. But I have to say, a spontaneous frog strangler occurring just after I whisper to Clara that I don't want to go to the lake? Coincidence? Ha!

CHAPTER
TWENTY-FOUR

I TAKE A LONG, SLOW bite out of *Quiche Your Face,* today's special. It's two thin pieces of bacon and spinach quiche acting like pieces of bread, with sharp cheddar cheese melted between them. Very messy. Very tasty. Very perfect for a rainy day.

"How do you like my experiment?" Mrs. Grant asks, rubbing her hands together like Doctor Frankenstein.

"I like it very much," I say. And I do. Its yumminess is distracting me from Taylor, who's standing just behind the curtains leading to the stairs. She's staring at me and I'm pretending I don't notice. I think of everything Twitch and I talked about, and how humans are lucky to be imperfect so we can keep trying new things. If he could forgive Clara for being such a terrible jerk, surely I can forgive Taylor, who wasn't *trying* to be jerk but was one accidentally.

I look over at her and our eyes lock. Her eyes squint as we look at each other, and her lips pucker into a frown. She flips her long hair as she whips around and stomps up the stairs. Well, maybe *now* she's trying to be a jerk? How did I go from being pretty sure I knew every thought in Taylor's head to now knowing zero things banging around in that mind of hers?

Mrs. Grant has seen all of this, of course, and sighs. "This might be partly my doing."

I look at her, startled. "How?"

"I told her about Rosalie the other day. And then I told her how, when I was young, I tried the Ouija board to contact her."

My mouth falls open. Mrs. Grant holds up a hand. "I didn't tell her to try that with you, I promise. But I'm afraid I gave her the idea. Also, she was upset that I told you about Rosalie but hadn't told her." She sighs again. "I guess I can't blame her for that."

The rain and my reprieve from having to go to the lake have put me in a good mood. I want Taylor to be in a good mood, too. I want to tell her that Clara made it rain. I want this stupid fight to be over.

"Don't let anyone eat this," I say, taking one more bite and jumping off my stool. "I'll be right back." Mrs. Grant nods as if, of course, someone would wander by and attempt to eat a partially eaten sandwich.

Before I'm even halfway up the stairs to the

apartment, Ratface is barking like I'm leading a herd of armed robbers to storm the building.

"I don't want to talk to anyone!" Taylor yells through the closed door at the top of the stairs. It sounds like Ratface is throwing his barks at the door.

"I'm not coming to talk to *you*!" I yell back. "I'm coming to talk to Ratface. He seems upset." I can hear him throwing *himself* now, bodily, up against the closed door. Tiny *thwumps* are like little commas between his barks. "I think he feels bad about the other day. Don't you, Ratface?" The more he hears his name, the more frenzied he gets. I know Taylor hates this, and even though I feel sort of guilty, I love that I'm riling him up. "Ratface wants to say he's sorry, doesn't he? Doesn't he?" I'm using my goofy talking-to-a-dog voice now, and Ratface's barks are turning from ANGRY STRANGER barks to *hellohelloyou'remyfriend* barks. "Don't you want to say you're sorry for ruining a top-notch plan to fool me into thinking my dead sister was communicating with me from beyond the grave? Don't you, Ratface?"

Ratface goes nuts, slamming into the door and barking. He's throwing in a couple of whines here and there, and I'm starting to feel bad for teasing him.

"Amelia—" Taylor's voice is calmer now. I hear her mutter, "Ratface, no!" She sounds closer to the door.

"Ratface, your voice sounds weirdly like Taylor's.

How do you do that?" He barks at me. "Did you want to say you're sorry, Ratface? Do you want to use Taylor's voice to say you're sorry?"

"Amelia, I—" Taylor starts to talk but there's a huge crash downstairs in the store.

What the heck?

I run down the stairs and see a bunch of people huddled by a collapsed display of homemade jams. Glass jars are shattered, and ones that aren't are rolling around. Someone is on the ground, but I can't see who because of all the other people. Someone yells, "Call nine-one-one!" just as I push through the people.

It's Mrs. Grant. She's on the ground, one arm splayed to the side, one leg bent in an impossible angle under her. There's a big goose egg growing on her head. Her eyes are closed. Her face is the same color as the old gray ashes in our fireplace. It is not a color a human should be.

"TAYLOR!" I scream, but she must have heard the crash, too. She's right behind me, phone already out. "She needs glucose," she says to herself and runs behind the counter. Ratface is at my feet, no longer barking. He runs to Mrs. Grant and licks her face over and over and over again like he's a prince and she's Sleeping Beauty and maybe enough of his kisses will wake her up.

A siren wails in the distance.

"Amelia." Mom's voice is quiet, and she's shaking my shoulder. "Honey, wake up." I struggle to surface from a dream. Her voice is like the light you can see when you're deep underwater, and I make my brain reach for it until my eyes slowly open. It takes a second for me to remember where we are.

The hospital.

I sit up straight, with a start. The waiting room is entirely empty except for me and Mom. Where are Taylor and her mom and dad?

"Did—" I start, feeling panic crash up through my chest like a tsunami.

Mom puts her hand softly but firmly on my arm. "Everything is okay. Taylor and her parents are in the room with Mrs. Grant. The doctors were able to stabilize her. Something happened with her blood sugar and she got dizzy and then hit her head when she fell. She's going to stay for a few days, but should be fine."

I wipe drool off my cheek from where my face had been smushed up against the armrest of my chair. How in the world did I manage to fall asleep while all of this was going on? "She's . . . Mrs. Grant . . . she's going to be okay?"

Mom nods and the tsunami of panic crashes over me as a wave of relief instead. She takes her hand off my arm and picks up her purse from where it's been leaning against her chair. "We should get home and get some rest. You have a big day tomorrow."

I stand up and rack my brain. Big day tomorrow? It's not my birthday. It's not Taylor's birthday. No exams at school.

"Softball tryouts," Mom says with a soft smile. "It's been written on the calendar for months."

Well, *now* I'm awake. With everything that's been going on, I guess I hadn't realized they were coming up so fast. Oh my gosh. Am I ready? Should I not do it because Mrs. Grant is sick and Taylor might need me here at the hospital? Is that just an excuse to not do it? I should do it. I mean, Clara made it rain for me, I should definitely get on the softball team for her. But . . . there's no way she made it rain. She doesn't exist anymore. So then, if I miss tryouts, it won't bother her. Because she wouldn't know. But I would know. I'm doing this for me, right? I look around for Taylor. I need her to talk me into this. I need her to remind me why I'm doing it. I'm breathing fast. Panicking.

"All that running. All that playing catch," Mom says, taking my hand as we walk out of the waiting room. "The brave sacrifice our kitchen window made on your behalf." Mom is quiet for a second. Then she says, "You've really put a lot into preparing for this, Amelia. I'm proud of you."

My panic disappears and I want so badly, all of a sudden, to tell Mom that I'm doing this for Clara; it's not really for me, I'm doing it because it's a goal Clara never got to achieve. But Mom is looking at me with such hope, her eyes are practically screaming, "HAL-LELUJAH, AMELIA IS DOING A THING NOR-MAL KIDS DO," that I can't bring myself to tell her.

The lights in the hallway are so bright they make me squint. Rooms on either side of us have closed doors but big windows so the nurses can see in. I try to look ahead and not into the rooms, even though I wonder about the people in each of the beds, and I also wonder about the people sitting in the chairs next to the beds, or about the empty chairs next to so many of them.

At the end of the hallway are double doors. Mom and I stand dumbly in front of them, waiting for them to open, but they don't. I push on them but they seem to be locked. Then I see there's a big square button on the wall you have to push to open them. I smash my hand into it right when I hear slapping feet running behind us. I turn around and it's Taylor, bare-foot, hair flying around her shoulders. She runs right into me and we both let out a little "*oof*" as we stum-ble into the button I just pushed, which pushes it again, closing the doors this time.

Taylor is squeezing me tightly, a hug to rival all hugs

before it. "I'm sorry," she whispers into my neck. I can feel her hot breath and damp cheeks. "I was stupid, and I'm sorry. I won't try to make you stop feeling sad and I won't ever stop being your friend."

I'm not sure what to say. Earlier today, *she* was the one who was mad at *me*. Am I also supposed to say I'm sorry?

"It's okay," I manage to say. "It's all okay. I'm not mad anymore. Are you mad at me?" Taylor releases me from her hug but doesn't let go of my arms. She pushes me away from her so she can look at me. Her blue eyes x-ray through me for a few seconds, and then she pulls me into another hug.

"I was mad at you for being mad at me. And I was jealous of Twitch. And then I found out Gram was pouring her heart out to you, and it felt like everyone was just pushing me away and leaving me out of everything. Like, no one even noticed I was alive anymore. But now none of that matters. It's all so stupid." She's crying into my neck again, and I don't think I've ever seen Taylor like this before. She's always the one who knows exactly what to do and say. She's always the one in control. She's never *ever* the invisible one. I hold on to her while she cries. We're still leaning on the button and the big doors keep opening and closing until a nurse gives us a look and Mom gently pushes us away from it.

"Ratface says he's sorry, too," Taylor says with a sniff.

"Well, I'm never forgiving him, so that's too bad," I say. Taylor laughs.

"Poor Ratface," she says. "He was only trying to help."

"All anyone is ever trying to do is help," I say. "Don't you think?"

Taylor nods. She pushes herself away from me and wipes her nose with the back of her hand. We look at each other for a minute and I start to feel a little embarrassed at so much emotion spilling out everywhere.

"Good luck at tryouts," Taylor says.

"Thanks," I say, deciding not to tell her I had actually forgotten about them until about five minutes ago.

"You're going to do great," she says. "Clara would be so proud."

Mom perks up at the mention of Clara and gives me a quizzical look.

"Tell Gram that we love her and hope she feels better so soon, it's really yesterday that she's feeling better."

Taylor laughs. "I will definitely tell her that. Good night, Amelia."

"Good night, Taylor," I say. We smile and it feels so good to not be mad anymore.

Mom punches the button and the doors open. We walk through and, as they start to close, Taylor yells after us, "Who run the world?"

"Girls!" I yell back.

She gives me a thumbs-up. "Kick butt tomorrow, Amelia."

The doors close, and I follow Mom through the lobby and out to the car.

CHAPTER TWENTY-FIVE

A CLOUD OF RED DIRT blows over my face as I lie on the ground, motionless, a slug drying in the sun.

"Peabody? Is that your name? You okay?" A girl leans over me, offering her hand. I grab it and she heaves me to my feet. "That was an epic miss, my friend," she says with a laugh. "But at least you committed." Several other girls are standing near us, trying not to laugh. A few more are actually laughing. The coach is off to the side, face squinched up like she's just smelled Ratface's breath.

"Sliding into first base is unnecessary," the coach says, walking over, "when the first baseman has already caught the ball and is standing on the bag."

My cheeks burn as I begin to realize that, maybe in addition to all the running and catching and throwing, I should have been learning the actual rules of how softball is played.

"Now," the coach says, walking away, "let's see who can throw."

After about fifteen minutes of watching incredibly athletic girls whip softballs into one another's gloves, I know the answer to this mystery: It Is Everyone But Peabody. I mean, it's not like I'm not trying, but good grief. I feel like a child among Olympians.

Coach finally tells us we can take a water break. I am covered in dirt and sweat and my arms might not ever work again. My hand shakes as I lift a paper cup of water to my lips.

"Amelia?" One of Coach's assistants, a girl who looks just like Twitch, but taller and prettier, comes up to me. She holds out her hand. "I'm Danielle, Billy's older sister."

I shake her hand. "I've been borrowing your glove a lot," I say because I don't know what else to say.

She nods as she looks me up and down, taking in my exhausted appearance. "And how's that been working out for you?"

I start to laugh. "Well, I'd heard it was a magical glove that made anyone who used it the best on the team. But maybe I've been using it wrong?"

Danielle laughs. "It's always made *me* the best on the team, so I'm not sure what to tell you." She winks as she walks away.

I look up at the blue sky and out at all the girls

running the bases. I imagine Clara out there shouting for the ball, throwing pitches, knocking home runs between the trees. She would have been good, I bet. Really good.

I crush up my paper cup, toss it into the metal trash can by the dugout, and walk over to the coach. "I think I'm going to leave now, if that's okay," I say, squinting up at her enormous frame.

She gives me a measured look. "If you give me time, I can turn you into a player." She pauses and taps her chin as she looks me up and down. "Probably."

I hold up my hand. "That's okay." I give her my glove. "Can you get this back to Danielle? I'm going to go home and take a shower."

Coach takes the glove and nods. "Nice effort, Peabody. Keep practicing. And, hey, maybe think about trying out for the high-school team next year."

"I probably won't do that," I say with a small laugh as I rub the growing bruise on my hip. "But thanks for your optimism."

Coach tips her hat and I walk away, limping, but only slightly.

CHAPTER
TWENTY-SIX

MRS. GRANT IS PROPPED UP in her hospital bed with a little wheeled table perched over her lap. Her glasses are on the end of her nose as she reads. I wave at Taylor through the window and her face visibly brightens when she sees me. She taps Mrs. Grant on the shoulder, and she looks up and waves me in.

I've come straight from tryouts, so I'm still super sweaty and covered in red dirt. I don't want to stay long, I just wanted to tell Taylor what happened.

"Well, you definitely smell really sporty," Taylor says, wrinkling her nose as I sit on the armrest of her chair. "How did it go?"

"Great!" I say. "I was so good the coach not only added me to the starting lineup, she made me captain."

Taylor's mouth hangs open in surprise. Mrs. Grant sets down her book and stares at me. I start to laugh.

"You should see your faces! Of course, she didn't make me captain. I left tryouts before they were even over." I stand up and slide my pants over my hip to show them the top of the bruise blooming from my misguided slide into first. "I'm not really cut out for sports."

Now they're both flinching. "Do you need some ice?" Mrs. Grant asks. "Taylor, get this girl some ice!" I wave them off.

"I'm fine," I say. "How are YOU?"

Mrs. Grant taps her chest and raises her eyebrows in a "who, me?" kind of way. I laugh. "You look pretty good. I mean, compared with yesterday when . . ." I make a "yikes" face.

"Oh, please tell me I didn't look like *that*," Mrs. Grant says. "I was imagining a more dignified concussion. At least with my mouth closed."

"You scared us," I say, remembering her on the floor. "A lot." She opens her arms and snaps her hands at me in a "come here" way. I stand and walk closer and she grabs me up in a hug. She feels solid and warm. I hold on for a very long time.

She lets go of me first and I acquiesce. I have to get home and shower and change so I can meet Twitch at Pits 'n' Pieces. Stupid lake. Maybe Clara will make it rain again. I look hopefully out the window facing the parking lot, but the sky continues to be bright blue and completely cloudless. Dang.

"I have to go," I say. "But I wanted to stop by and see how you were doing. And to tell you to feel better."

"I'll be out of here faster than Ratface can eat a dropped hot dog." Mrs. Grant smiles.

Taylor stands. "I'll walk you out. Be back in a second, Gram." Mrs. Grant nods. She's already back to whatever it was she was reading on the little table. Taylor and I walk out into the hall, through the doors, and to the lobby.

"We haven't really talked a lot about the prank," Taylor says.

"I know," I say, looking at my feet. "And we're running out of time."

Taylor swallows hard and looks over my shoulder, avoiding eye contact. "Lacy and Katherine and I . . . well . . ."

"It's okay," I say. "Do the prank with them. I'll figure something out."

"But—" Taylor looks at me now. Her face is a mixture of relief and something else. Sadness? Oh, it better not be pity. I feel my eyes go squinty as Taylor says, "I don't want to abandon you, Amelia. You'll have to do one all alone. Why don't you just join us?"

"It's fine," I say. And it really is. I'd rather do it by myself than join a group that only wants me because they'd feel bad about themselves if they didn't offer an invitation. "I have a million ideas."

Taylor looks at me with only relief now. "Good! I mean, I'm sorry that I kind of went rogue on this, but . . ."

"Don't worry about it," I say. "Things got weird and Prank Day is coming up. I get it." I do get it. I still feel a smidge of a sting that she joined a group without telling me, but having a conversation like this in the lobby of a hospital where people are waiting for surgery and crying about terrible things and all of that . . . it puts stuff like school pranks into perspective, you know?

"See you at school tomorrow?" Taylor asks as I make my way to the sliding glass doors.

"Yep," I say. I walk outside and the blue sky is welcoming at first, such a contrast to the inside of the hospital. But then I remember what the rest of the day holds, and suddenly I can't even really think about the stupid prank anymore. The lake is looming in my future. I wonder how slowly I can walk home. I wonder how slowly I can shower and change. Maybe by the time I'm done it'll be dark and Pits 'n' Pieces will be closed. I sigh. That won't work, because then I'll just have to go tomorrow.

I look down the sidewalk like it's the longest pirate plank in the world.

CHAPTER
TWENTY-SEVEN

THE LAKE RIPPLES IN THE breeze. The trees along its edges are the kind of green that seems to pulse with life. It's a beautiful Saturday. The sun is warm on my face, and I close my eyes for a second so I can soak it up. The redness of the inside of my eyelids makes me remember Taylor's kitchen and the Ouija board, which makes my eyes snap open. The sun glinting off the shiny silver of the Pits 'n' Pieces Airstream is so bright I think it might burn through my corneas. The line in front of the window is about ten people deep. Dad must be loving this.

I walk past Thai Me Up, Thai Me Down—the Thai food trailer that won the Best Almost Fast Food award last year. Their line is pretty long, too. Next, I pass Leafy Queens, a salad trailer. I actually like the black bean salad they serve, but I'd never tell Dad. He thinks salads are only good for rabbits and feeding compost bins.

Behind Pits 'n' Pieces, Twitch is adding wood to one of the smokers.

"Hey," I say. He's sweaty and wearing big gloves to protect his hands from the mesquite splinters.

"Hey," he says. "You're late."

"Well, technically, *I* didn't break the window."

He gives me a frowny look, but then smiles. "Nice try, Peabody. Last I remember, you're the one who couldn't catch." He stands up straight and his eyes get big. "Oh! How were tryouts?"

I start to laugh. I can tell from his ridiculous face he already knows. "Did Danielle tell you?"

He reaches under his crooked helmet and scratches his head—he's trying so hard to pretend he doesn't know anything. "Uh," he says. "No. I just . . . how did . . ." He looks more and more uncomfortable the more I laugh.

"It was awful!" I shout at him. "Twitch. You should have seen it. I flopped around like a Muppet."

Now he's laughing, too. "Danielle said you had a lot of heart."

I punch him in the shoulder. "That's what they say about people who are TERRIBLE," I snort.

"It is indeed," he says, punching me back, but much softer than I punched him.

"What!" Dad yells out the little back door of the trailer, "is going ON out there?! Amelia! Come help me! I'm drowning in here!"

Time slows to a pinpoint as we all hear what he just said.

I swear I can hear the lake laughing.

Dad blinks once. Twice. And time goes back to normal again. "Can you just get up here and help me?" he asks, voice softer now. "If we're this busy now," he mutters under his breath, "I can't even imagine how it might be if we win that contest." His brow is wrinkled. It's the first time I've seen Dad look really stressed out in a long time.

I nod and run up the stairs after him. Only then does it strike me that for the few minutes Twitch and I were talking I completely forgot that we were even at the lake, and what the lake means.

But now, as I stand beside Dad, filling cups with barbecue sauce and looking out the windows onto the lake, it's like I've been taken back in time. Of course, Dad didn't have the trailer then. We were just normal people having a normal birthday party at the lake, like the people I can see today, down by the water's edge tying balloons onto a picnic table and setting up coolers.

I wore my yellow swimsuit, the one I thought made me swim faster. Clara was wearing a two-piece with big red flowers on it. Her hair was jet black and scraggly at the ends because neither one of us had had haircuts in ages. Her skin was so brown from all the days

we'd spent in the sun, it made the colors of her swimsuit pop.

"I hate you!" I screamed at her. "I never want to see
you again!"

Those were my last words to my sister, as she stuck
her tongue out at me and zoomed away on the boat
full of her friends. Those were the last words she ever
heard out of my mouth.

"Pulled pork sandwich and potato salad." I hear a
familiar voice, and it snaps me back to the moment. It's
Desiree, Twitch's friend from the woods. She's wearing
those giant hoop earrings again and they shine in the
sun. Gathered around her are Maureen and Henry and
Jake. Everyone from the boat that day. Everyone from
the woods.

"Hey, Amelia," Jake says, running his hands through
his curly hair. "Twitch said you guys were going to be
up here today. We thought we'd come up for lunch.
And, you know . . ."

"For support," Maureen finishes for him. "The lake
can be, I don't know . . ."

"Kind of hard to deal with," Henry finishes for her.
Desiree nods.

Twitch comes around from the back of the trailer
and sees them. "Heeeeeeeey!" he shouts. "You came!"
They all awkwardly group-hug. Dad looks at me and
at them. The line behind them is really long.

"Go out there for a second," Dad says. "But then get back in here." He swipes really quickly at his bright eyes. I guess Dad must remember them from that day, too. How could he not? It's a day emblazoned on all of our brains. Every detail. Every second. Seared in there forever.

I run out the back of the trailer and around front and join in the awkward hug. "I can't believe you all came out here," I say into the pile of armpits surrounding my face.

"We're all in this together, kiddo," Desiree says. "At least, now we are." She tightens her arm around my shoulder and it feels really, really good to feel really, really sad with other people. Isn't that weird? How can a person feel good and sad at the same time? It's like these guys have created some kind of new way to feel inside of me. Happysad. An accidental gift.

"Pulled pork and potato salad!" Dad yells from the window, holding a paper plate full of food. "One for everyone." He hands plates down to me, and I hand them to Clara's friends. My friends, now. Henry pulls out some cash, but Dad waves him off. "Just tell everyone you know it's the best barbecue you've had in your entire life."

"Deal, Mr. Peabody," Jake says, mouth full of sandwich. They all make their way to a picnic table nearby as Twitch and I walk back around the trailer.

Twitch smiles at me as I go up the little stairs. "I thought they might help the day go by a bit easier."

"Well, you thought right," I say, smiling back.

And it works. Every time I look out the window and see the lake looming, I also see Maureen and Desiree, Jake and Henry, camped at the picnic table playing cards, goofing around, or waving back at me and Twitch. I still don't love being at the lake, but I've stopped feeling the horrible dread and gloom that I did on my way over here.

Finally, Dad puts out the CLOSED sign, and Twitch and I help clean up everything for the night. "If the day of the TV show goes anything like today, we have first place in the bag," Dad says. He pulls at his beard, and his eyes look out over the water. After a minute, he snaps back to reality and says, "Winning that contest could really change things." For just a blink of a second his eyes seem kind of sad, then he brightens and smiles at us. "Who's ready for bed?"

"It's eight thirty, Mr. Peabody," Twitch says.

"Exactly," Dad answers, and we all laugh as we head to the car.

CHAPTER
TWENTY-EIGHT

"HEY," I SAY, KNOCKING ON Mom and Dad's bedroom door. Mom is in bed with her glasses on and a bunch of paperwork spread around her. She looks up. Her laptop is on her lap, and its glowing screen reflects in her glasses. Dad must be downstairs watching TV.

"Hey, Amelia. What's up?" She slides a bunch of papers out of the way and pats the bed next to her. I sit down, awkwardly at first, but then I lean back on her inclined pillows next to her and I have a flash of memory from when I was little and used to climb into bed with Mom and Dad after a bad dream. Without even thinking about it, I tilt my head until it rests on her shoulder. She tucks my hair behind my ear, like she used to, and pushes her glasses up onto her head like they're a headband.

"Seriously," she says, "what's going on?"

For a second, I want to tell her about the letter. I want to tell her about softball. I want to tell her about the art project in the woods. I want to tell her everything. But there's so much to tell I can't find the words. I don't know where to start. I don't even really know why I suddenly want to tell her all this stuff right now. That's not why I came in here. But with my head on her shoulder, and her Mom smell reminding me of when I was little and when things were simpler, I don't know. I guess . . . I'm just really, really aware all of a sudden of how tired I am. Not like in a sleepy way, but in an everything way. I feel like I'm always swimming upstream. I'm always trying to push my way through things instead of just being carried along. I want things to be easy again, like they were when Clara was alive. Back when I didn't even know things were easy.

"I'm thinking about my prank," I say, which is about one-ninety-ninth of all the things I'm thinking about. "Do you know who's in charge of deciding how public art gets money?" Mom turns to face me, making me have to lift my head from her shoulder. She blinks. I don't think she thought this is what I was going to ask.

"Well," she starts. "Grace McNeil oversees the distribution of public funds, but she's not the one who makes the final decisions. Often there's a town vote if the funds are going toward something that isn't already a budget line item."

I hear her words, but they don't make a lot of sense, so I start over. "I have some friends who made this really cool art project. They're trying to figure out how to, like, protect it and turn it into something the whole public can enjoy. I was thinking maybe I could use their art as part of my prank. Or something." The truth is, I haven't really thought out much of anything. But I would like to help them get the money they need to preserve their art. "How can they turn their art into something for everyone?"

Mom scrunches up her face. "Unsanctioned public art? Is that what you're getting at? This sounds a little bit like you're talking about vandalism. You know vandalism is against the rules for Prank Day."

"It's not vandalism," I say, and my usual irritated-with-Mom feelings start rising to the surface. She gives me a look like she's not sure she believes me, but then goes into minute detail about grants and permissions and land ownership and all sorts of things that sound super boring. While she's talking, it hits me. I know *exactly* what to do with the art project. I know *exactly* how to turn it into something public without having to jump through all those hoops.

"You look excited," Mom says, interrupting herself

in mid-sentence. "I had no idea you have such a passion for small-town bureaucracy."

I jump up and kiss her on the forehead. "Thanks, Mom!" and I run back to my room to start planning.

All I need is a saw that can carefully slice concrete, the ability to lift super-heavy slabs, some kind of flatbed truck . . . aaargh. I drop my head on my desk. This isn't going to work at all. But there has to be *some* way . . . if I can figure out how to move the artwork from the woods and get it to the fountain, this will be the best prank ever in the history of pranks.

I slip on my jacket and tiptoe downstairs. I ease the kitchen door open as slowly as possible so it doesn't squeak, and walk as lightly as I can across the porch, down the little stairs, and onto the driveway. I look over my shoulder. No one is chasing after me, so I think my escape worked. I jog down the street until I see the lights of the town square, and I slow to a walk. It's pretty late, so not many people are out.

I sit on the edge of the broken fountain and give it a long, hard look. It's tiered, kind of like a cake, with a small circle on top in the shape of a very shallow bowl, a larger circle-bowl in the center, and then the big basin at the bottom. Shooting out of the top bowl is a giant bird with its mouth wide open. I guess years and years ago water shot out of the bird's mouth and cascaded down into the lower circle, where it over-flowed into the basin. The basin is about knee-deep and maybe twelve feet in diameter.

I briefly imagine having some kind of magical skills to break up and transport the art project to the foun-tain, and then reassemble it in the basin of the fountain. I sigh. Yeah, there's no way I'm going to be able to do that. For one thing, the art wouldn't fit. For another, I don't think there's any way to move it. For another, even if there was a way to move it, it would weigh like 5,735,385,753 pounds.

BUT. What if I re-create the art, and add a little something extra?

I look around to see if anyone can see me, but the town square is deserted. I climb into the empty basin, rub my hands together, and reach up onto the middle circle, pulling myself up and hanging on by my elbows for a second. Then I heave myself up until I'm stand-ing on it. I can just barely peer into the bird's mouth, but it's really dark in there. I think I can see some kind of piping going way down, which would make sense. The pipe would have to recirculate water from the basin up into the bird's mouth so that it would shoot out and keep the fountain going. What if . . . My mind is really spinning now. As long as the piping from the basin to the bird's mouth isn't broken, or there's room for a hose, I might be able to . . . My heart leaps and I laugh out loud. If I can manage this prank, it might be the best prank ever AND it might be the perfect public art to complement the project in the woods. I leap down into the basin, hop over the edge, and run to Twitch's house.

It's late, so I don't bother going to the front door. I throw a handful of pebbles at his bedroom window like he did to mine. A few seconds later, the window rises and he looks down at me. He's wearing a T-shirt that's ripped along the neck.

"Amelia? What are you doing down there?"

"I just had the best idea!" I whispershout up at him.

"It's eleven o'clock at night!" he whispershouts back. "Have you not heard of phones?" But he's smiling, so I know he isn't mad.

"Come down here for a second!" I say.

He gives me an exasperated look but closes the window. In a minute, he's standing in the grass next to me and I'm asking him if he has any paint left over. His smile grows wider and wider as I explain how we can turn the fountain into a mirror of the art in the woods. "I love it," he whispers. "I'm sure we can do it. We have to tell the rest of the crew."

I nod and smile, so excited.

Twitch holds up a finger. "I think we can text them, though. Let's not get busted the first night out, okay?"

I nod again and pull my phone from my pocket.

Twitch tells me everyone's numbers and I send out a group text. We both watch as my phone blows up with responses. Everyone is in.

This is going to be the best prank in the history of eighth-grade pranks. .

CHAPTER
TWENTY-NINE

THE NEXT FEW DAYS ARE a blur. Twitch's crew and I have spent hours in the town library, and our hands are cramped from so much work with scissors. We've gathered all the paint we need, and now we're all lying on the floor in my bedroom trying to take a quick nap before the sun goes down. Tomorrow is Prank Day and we're going to need the whole night to finish. Tomorrow is also the day they film *Trailer Takeout*, because of course. I've barely seen Mom or Dad in days. I have no idea how they're going to be able to see my prank and how I'm going to get down to the trailer for the contest. We'll just have to wing it, I guess.

I'm not sure if anyone has actually slept at all, but we've been quiet as the light has moved from the top of my window to the bottom of it, casting the room in a light orange, evening glow. Mom knocks on the doorframe (the door is open because GIRLS AND BOYS

IN ONE ROOM AHH NIGHTMARE SCENARIO),
and she's holding a big brown bag covered in grease
stains.

"Sausages and fries?" she asks. "Before the big
night out?"

We all sit up, looking kind of groggy. Mom sets the
bag on the floor in the middle of us and puts down a
roll of paper towels. She disappears and comes back
with a twelve-pack of soda and a smile.

"I hope Amelia has told you all thank you for helping her this week," Mom says, and I can't help but roll
my eyes.

"Oh, Mrs. Peabody," Desiree says with a genuine
smile. "Amelia is the one who has been helping us."

Mom doesn't seem to know what to say to that, so
she gives me a quizzical look as she backs out of the
room. Then she disappears down the stairs.

"Music?" Twitch asks, hooking his phone up to my
speakers. Something bouncy and thwumpy plays, and
we all get up and dance while we eat our sausages and
fries. It's all so silly and spontaneous . . . and fun.

"Hey!" I shout. "Am I having a party right now?"

"I don't know!" Jake shouts back. "It kind of feels
like a party." He offers up his soda and we all yell,
"Cheers!" as we crash our cans together.

I set down my food and drink and pull Clara's letter
from my pocket.

4) *Throw an awesome birthday party on the lake.* *(Invite everyone, make sure the boat is working, have enough ice cream for the whole town, make sure everyone knows it's YOU, Most Beautiful Queen of the Universe, in charge.)*

I look up at everyone laughing and dancing in my room. It's no one's birthday, and we're definitely not at the lake, and sausages are not ice cream, and yet . . . this totally counts as a party. I cross number four off the list.

"What's that?" Mom stares over my shoulder. I hadn't heard her come back in my room. She's holding a box of cookies, but she sets it down on my dresser as she leans closer.

"Is that . . . ?" she says, her voice quiet.

"Clara's," I finish for her. "Mrs. Henderson accidentally gave me Clara's letter at the beginning of the school year instead of mine. I've been trying to do all the things she never got to do." The music is still thumping, but no one is dancing anymore.

"Oh, Amelia," Mom says. "Oh, honey." She grabs me up in a hug. And suddenly everyone is hugging us. It's an enormous group hug with lots of sniffles. After a few minutes, we break apart and I hand the letter to Mom so she can see it better. She reads over it, then takes my pen and scratches off number one, the part that says "be nicer to Mom and Amelia."

"Looks like you've completed the list," she says, kissing me on the top of my head.

"Hey, guys," Twitch says. "I hate to interrupt, but it's eight o'clock. We need to get going!" We all scramble around to grab our supplies. I'm the last out of my room, with Mom beside me. She hugs me again and says, "You're a wonder, Amelia."

Those are really nice words to hear.

CHAPTER THIRTY

THE SUN IS JUST STARTING to rise, painting the sky in beautiful orange and pink streaks, when we finish. The fast-drying paint is a little bit sticky still, but not enough to smear. We've checked and rechecked the tubing, and set up the table next to us with golden paper, pens, and scissors. The Clara Peabody Memorial Stardust Fountain is ready for business.

We've painted the inside of the fountain a deep, dark blue, just like the project in the woods. The edges of the basin are painted red and jaggedy white, just like the project, too. And as for the stars . . . my fingers are crossed that it's going to work.

People are starting to gather around the fountain now, because everyone in town gets up early on Prank Day to see what's new and crazy. It's a town tradition, and I think some people look forward to it more than Christmas. You never know what's going to come from the minds of eighth graders given free rein, and as long as it isn't destructive or dangerous, everyone cheers us on. I hope they don't count painting the fountain as destructive, but I guess we can always paint it white again if they make us.

I look at Twitch, who nods. Desiree and Henry give me a thumbs-up, and Maureen and Jake smile encouragingly. I lean down to the hole next to the fountain where we've rigged our tubing and a small but superstrong fan. At the end of the tube I attach a huge plastic bag filled with golden stars cut from fancy paper. I put the fan (still turned off) in the other end of the bag and secure the edges so none of the stars can fall out. The crowd is bigger now, murmuring and looking at the painted fountain.

I flip the fan's switch and it turns on with a forceful whir, blowing the stars from the bag up through the tubing. I'm afraid they've all jammed up in there and gotten caught, but then stars begin to shoot out of the bird's mouth, gold catching the early morning sun and glimmering bright.

Everyone in the crowd sucks in their breath at the same time as the beauty of the gold stars flutters overhead. Maureen is by the bag now, filling it with more and more stars. They're flying out of the bird's mouth and into the air, some landing in the fountain, but others landing in people's hair or on their shoulders or their shoes. It's like snow, but with stars. I can't help but laugh out loud with the joy of the moment. It worked! My idea worked!

I hear someone say, "What's this?" A woman is looking at a star and trying to make out the words we carefully wrote on each of them.

"Every star has a name on it," I say. "Each star is for a person who lived here in town at some point in history but has now passed on. If there's a person you'd like to add, we have a table here with pens and papers and scissors. You can make your own stardust for the people you love. They don't have to have lived here, they can be from anywhere."

Mrs. Grant hands me a paper cup of hot tea and puts her arm around my shoulder. She squeezes tight. "This is beautiful, Amelia. Just beautiful."

I reach into my pocket and hand her a star. On it, I've written *Rosalie* in my best handwriting. Mrs. Grant takes the star and kisses me on the forehead. She goes to Maureen and puts it in the bag so that it can fly out of the bird's mouth, making Rosalie part of our stardust morning.

I see my parents in the crowd, and I feel this huge relief that they made it! I was so afraid they might miss the fountain because of the contest. Their faces are pointed at the sky, small stars falling all around them, smiling. I go over to them and hug them both. "I fixed what you broke, Dad."

Dad's eyes fly open. "How did you—"

"You told Clara, and she told me," I say.

"That stinker! She wasn't supposed to tell anyone."

"Well, technically, I guess, she didn't," I say, digging in my pocket for her letter. I show it to Dad. His face goes from happy to happysad as he reads it. He carefully folds it up and hands it back to me.

"Mom told me you had this, but I didn't know she mentioned the fountain." His eyes are shiny bright.

"So, how did you break it?" I ask.

"We filled it with concrete," he says. "It was a dumb idea. We thought watery concrete would come out of the bird's mouth and harden so there would always be a stream of 'water' coming from its mouth. Instead, we mucked up all the piping. But it looks like you fixed it?" His bright eyes are now big with wonder.

"No," I say. "We couldn't get anything to work with those pipes, but there was enough room next to them to snake in some tubing of our own."

"Quite ingenious," Mom says.

I smile. The stars continue to fly around us.

Mom and Dad both grab me up in a big hug. "We hate to do this, Amelia, but Mom and I need to run," Dad says, looking at his watch. "Filming starts in half an hour and I'm sure everyone down there is freaking out that we aren't already there."

"We'll see you later?" Mom asks.

Before I can answer, Taylor runs up to us, out of breath. "You did all of this? Whoa, Amelia, it's gorgeous!"

"I had a lot of help," I say, gesturing to the crew. "These guys made it all possible, for sure."

Mom and Dad wave as they run to Old Betsy. I wave back.

"It's stunning," Taylor says, lifting her face to the falling stars. "Amazing."

"Where's your prank?" I ask. "What did you do?"

Taylor waves her hand dismissively. "Lacy wanted to find a bunch of chickens and let them loose in Town Square and have a 'Running of the Chickens' day, like the running of the bulls in Spain. But the chickens all just stood around pecking the ground, and none of them would go anywhere."

"Points for effort?" I say with a laugh.

Taylor laughs, too. "No points for anything. Except, all the chickens are still alive—and well fed. So, I guess maybe points for that?"

Hours go by as people wander over and marvel at the stardust fountain. Some people smile big, some cry a little. It's kind of like a giant bonding moment for the whole town.

Mrs. Grant brings over drinks and snacks, and I remember—*bam*—I need to get down to Pits 'n' Pieces!

"Do you guys think you can keep helping out for a little bit?" I ask everyone. "I have to go help with the TV show stuff." And even though I know they all have to be just as tired as I am, everyone shouts out, "You bet!" and "No problem!" and "Good luck!"

Mrs. Grant jangles her car keys. "William, can you take Amelia to the lake? And not wreck my car?"

"Yes, ma'am," Twitch says, his face very serious. Mrs. Grant points at her car parked in the alley by the General Store. It's about a thousand years old and looks like it's held together with duct tape.

"I'll try not to wreck it any more than it's already wrecked." Twitch winks at her and she slaps his arm before she hands over her keys.

"I mean it!" she says. "Not a scratch."

"Do you think they'll let us keep the fountain like this? Forever?" I ask Mrs. Grant, even though I know she doesn't know. "Like a monument to everyone's loved ones?"

"I don't know," Mrs. Grant says. "But you should definitely ask."

She kisses my cheek, and then Twitch and I run to the car.

CHAPTER THIRTY-ONE

"HOW'S THAT POTATO SALAD COMING along?" Dad asks. The TV show crew are outside the trailer taking video of the line. I finish stirring the big pot, cover it with plastic wrap, and push it into the fridge. "It's going to be great. Best potato salad ever." I've never made potato salad before, but Dad was insistent that today was the big day . . . today was going to be the first day of my potato salad reign.

Mom is in the cramped corner mixing cookie dough at Dad's request, which is hilarious because I'm not sure she's ever actually worked *in* the trailer before. Sure, she helps Dad stock stuff and set things up and whatever, but she always said she'd never set foot inside the trailer as an employee. "This is your thing," she'd say, pointing at Dad. "Yours." But today he weirdly asked for help cooking, and the two of us said okay. I guess we both know how important this is to him.

Dad strokes his beard nervously. "I know I keep saying this, but if we win this thing, it could really change our lives. I would probably have to start a real restaurant, or buy a few more trailers and put them in other towns. Our popularity would skyrocket. And so would my workload."

I look at him and tilt my head to the side, like he does to me when he isn't sure he understands what I'm saying. "Do you want that, though?" I ask. "I thought you liked having the small trailer and experimenting with flavors and stuff. I didn't think you wanted to go corporate, or whatever."

Dad tugs his beard some more, wrinkles getting deeper at the sides of his eyes as he smiles at me. "How did you get to be so smart?"

"Must be in the genes," Twitch says, coming up the small stairs into the trailer. He goes to the sink in the back and washes his hands. "The crowd out there is huge. I thought you might need a hand."

"The crowd in *here* is huge," Mom says. And she's right. Four people inside this trailer is super-close quarters.

"Tell you what," Dad says. "Let's all agree right now that it doesn't matter if we win. The only things that matter are flavor and fun. Deal?"

Twitch and I both smile big. So does Mom. "Deal," we all say together.

"Jen, why don't you give me the cookie dough and go outside to take orders." Dad takes the bowl from Mom, who's face goes slack with relief.

"Excellent," she says. "I'm outta here." She grabs an order pad from the counter and thumps down the stairs.

With more room in the trailer, Dad, Twitch, and I become a well-oiled machine. The afternoon is a blur of crowds and cameras. People interview us over and over and take all kinds of video of us cooking and handing out plates of food and tossing wood into the smokers and a million other things. By sunset, Dad, Mom, Twitch, and I are all sweaty and smoky and exhausted.

Producer Stacy comes over, headphones dangling around her neck. "Ready to come outside? We're going to announce the winners."

We all climb out of the trailer and follow her to the beachy part of the lake. She makes us stand in the sandy dirt with our backs facing the water while she sets up the cameras. The Thai Me Up, Thai Me Down guys are here, too, and the Leafy Queens folks. We all wave to one another. No one really seems to care who wins, we're all so exhausted.

After what feels like forever, the host of the show

bounds over to us, all smiles and full of energy. He announces that—drumroll, please—Pits 'n' Pieces has been disqualified.

What!

Everyone stares at him.

Apparently, because I helped make the potato salad, and Mom helped with the cookies, and neither of our names was on the chef roster, our team has been disqualified from the competition. Thai Me Up, Thai Me Down is the winner.

What!

What!

Dad laughs really hard and pats me on the back. Mom's eyes are huge, but then they narrow and she smiles. She turns to Dad, and they share a glance before she pushes him hard in the shoulder and they both laugh. Did Dad *know* we were going to get disqualified? Twitch looks at me and I shrug.

Stacy jogs over to us once the cameras are off and being packed away. "You knew the rules. I remember going over them with you. So, why did you throw it?" she asks Dad. "You would have won, hands down, you know."

He shrugs.

"Having my family cook with me makes me feel like the big winner," he says. "Everyone together, having fun . . . at the lake." He throws his arm over my shoulder and gives me a squeeze. "That's the prize I wanted, and that's the prize I got."

"You!" I wiggle away and point at Dad. "You *knew* you were disqualifying us?! Dad! You sacrificed the contest just to get us to the lake?"

"It was a game-time decision," he said. "I don't need a restaurant. I don't need more trailers. I don't need to work myself to a nub. I have everything I need right here." He grabs me up in a big hug, and then drags Mom into it, too. After a second, he even grabs Twitch. "Now let's go swimming," he says. And before I can say or do anything, he runs from the sand, onto the wooden pier, and cannonballs into the lake. Twitch lets out a hoot and runs after him, doing the same thing. Then *Mom* gives a yell and flings herself off the pier. What! Ha! Before I can even believe what I'm doing, I run after them, too, leaping from the scratchy end of the dock, feeling the wind whip at my hair and then the freezing water engulf my body. I open my eyes underwater and see Dad still down there, his eyes open, too. He smiles and waves and then grabs Mom and hugs her from behind. She opens her eyes and makes a goofy underwater face. I smile and wave. Twitch does a handstand, before floating to the surface. It's all so silly, this wild underwater tableau. We all swim up to the surface and shake the water from our hair and ears.

Dad is in the lake.

Mom is in the lake.

Twitch is in the lake.

I'm in the lake.

And it isn't eating any of us.

There are a bunch of splashes and suddenly Maureen and Desiree and Jake and Henry are in the lake, too. Where did they come from? Then Mrs. Grant and Taylor come flying into the water and we're all laughing and spluttering and splashing.

"We ran out of paper, so we shut down the fountain . . . for now . . ." Mrs. Grant says, her white hair shimmering like a mermaid's. "I hope that's okay."

I can only smile and look around me. We're all in the lake, laughing and splashing and smiling. The sky is a deep, deep blue and the sun is setting behind the trees. The first stars of the night begin to twinkle overhead, leaving just a hint of stardust in our hair.

ACKNOWLEDGMENTS

Writing a book is such an interesting phenomenon. You're alone for much of the process, but you're also surrounded by the characters you've created. You technically spend your days by yourself—but having conversations and arguments, solving problems and going on adventures, making discoveries and amends. And then . . . your story is done. You turn it in to your editor and your brain is quiet and alone again. Except, you're *not* alone. There's a whole team who springs to life to bring your book to readers. Agents, editors, designers, copy editors, marketing whizzes, public relations teams, and more. But while they're all working you're . . . by yourself. Your characters have been whisked away and you no longer visit their towns and adventures every day, because everything is off being polished and perfected.

All this to say, being a writer is not an easy job. It's arguably one of the best jobs in the world, but it's hard. And when you have a hard, sometimes lonely, job you have to learn to trust other people to help you out. Some of the people who help me every day are Samuel and Georgia and Isaac. They know that I sometimes have to live in my head and in my heart, and that means dinner might be late or burned. The school field trip might be missed. They know I will have to leave them sometimes so I can visit other children and talk about my books. They know this, but they don't complain. (Well, sometimes they complain, but mostly about my terrible cooking.) My kids are my confidants, my beta readers, my support staff, my champions, and my heart. I love them dearly, and I'm not sure they always realize they are the top notch number one most important team members in getting *all* of my books written and published.

It's also imperative, when you're a writer, to have a whip-smart publishing team who seems to miraculously know how to get things just right. From editing to design to marketing to everything in between, I could not be luckier to be working with the team at Scholastic. Erin Black seems to live in my brain. Sometimes I think she sees my words before I do. (I hope she does, because when we're on the phone talking about a project, I get so excited I talk right over her and I have to depend on magic for her to understand me.) Melissa Schirmer is a brilliant production editor, keeping everything in line and in tip-top shape, and Baily Crawford has reached into my heart and created a design that can't be surpassed.

My agent, Ammi-Joan Paquette, deserves confetti cannons and jubilant trombone salutes for all of her hard work. She never asks "why" and always asks "why not," which keeps me constantly on my toes. Joan gives me confidence, which gives me freedom to write. Joan also gives me brutal truth, which gives me freedom to write *better*.

And to Shannon, my love. You are my stars and sunshine, my first thought every morning and my last thought every night. You believe in me, and that makes *me* believe in me. Every day I wonder where you came from. Maybe science can't prove fate, but maybe it doesn't need to.

ABOUT THE AUTHOR

Kari Anne Holt is the author of several books for young readers, including *House Arrest* and *Rhyme Schemer*, each of which was a Bank Street Best Book of the Year, and *Gnome-a-Geddon*. Dreaming up sandwiches with punny names and barbeque sauces she'd like to try are just a couple of her hobbies. Kari Anne lives in Austin, Texas, with her family, and you can find her online at www.KAHolt.com.